BRAiN RIDE

Angela Welch Prusia
Cyndi Mayer, Illustrator

BRAiN RIDE

Summary: When 14-year-old Logan suffers a traumatic brain injury, circumstances threaten to destroy his friendship with best friend, Jason, so the two boys reluctantly agree to train for an organized bike ride which takes them on the ride of their lives.

ISBN 9781938478130

Printed in USA by Good Book Printing
www.goodbookprinting.com

Logan

Cow eyeballs.

The words bubble to the surface of my mind like Coke fizz. Mr. Bertholf leans against the rail of my hospital bed. His lips move, but the words are jumbled. The memory comes to me in fits, like a tantrum from my little sister.

Mr. Bertholf's science class. Sixth grade. Two years ago. Jason and I sit on lab stools, hovered over the specimen we're about to dissect. A large cow eyeball studies us without blinking.

"Dude, it looks like one of those monster jawbreakers," Jason snorts.

"So lick it," I dare him.

Jason flips me off with a gloved hand, and I laugh. Mr. Bertholf looks in our direction, but continues teaching.

"Make the first incision here." He points to a diagram on the whiteboard. Mr. Bertholf is so cool. What other teacher would bring cow eyeballs to class?

I grab the scalpel and slice through the cornea. I cringe, expecting blood to spurt out, but it doesn't. Wild.

Jason makes a face when I pull out the lens. "Cool. That's disgusting."

I roll the lens between my thumb and forefinger. It feels like a jelly bean that's been chewed.

"Logan? Logan?" Someone calls out my name from a distance.

I'm staring into Mr. Bertholf's face, but I'm not in science class. I shift my eyes to take in my surroundings. Slowly my brain registers the information.

I'm not in school. I'm in bed. A hospital bed in the ICU. Doc says I banged up my head real bad in a bike accident. They say I just woke up from a coma, but I don't remember anything. I'm hooked up to a machine that helps me breathe. Meds pump into me through an IV.

Jason is here. He never leaves. Mr. Bertholf smiles. He hands me a package, but I don't know what to do.

"Open it." Mr. Bertholf taps the top.

I fumble with the box, so Mr. Bertholf lifts the lid. He pulls something out. The thing looks familiar, but I can't remember what it's called. My head aches. It's so much work to think. Thinking's like breathing. You just do it. Until you can't. Like me.

Mr. Bertholf says something, but I lose most of the sentence. One word sticks out. "Helmet." I latch onto the word. Mr. Bertholf brought me a bike helmet.

I start to say something, but the words clump in my throat like a hairball. Mr. Bertholf squeezes my hand. "For when you ride again."

I never wore a helmet before. Why would I start now?

Jason

June 16

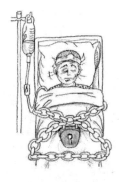

Score. I make the trashcan next to Logan's hospital door. Two points.

"What's this?" Mr. B walks into the room and plucks my wadded up sketch from the trash.

"Nothing."

He flattens it out and studies the picture. "You did this?"

I shrug. It's supposed to be Logan chained to his hospital bed. "Yeah."

Mr. B raises his eyebrows. "You're good."

I don't know what to say. Most people don't look past the clothes or the skateboard.

Logan

I stare at the mirror. My face is shredded with road rash, and I lost a couple teeth. Jet black hair pokes out of my scalp like one of my sister's Barbies after I gave it a whack job. Mom's always ragging on me to get a haircut, but now I look like an idiot. A nurse shaved my hair before the surgery to reduce the pressure in my head. My earring's gone, and they cut off my clothes, so I have to wear this stupid hospital gown. I'd kill for my jeans and a black t-shirt.

My stunts have landed me in the hospital before. Broken arm, busted collarbone, shattered ankle. Give it eight weeks and broken limbs heal. So I hit my head. Big deal. How's this any different? I'm already off the breathing machine.

Maybe a cast won't work, but they have neck braces. Get me a head support for a couple weeks, and I'll take it easy. No tricks on my bike. No skateboarding. No stunts on the ATV. I'll be good IF everybody would just quit freaking out. I promise.

I'm going to be fine. I get smacked around a lot. I'm not exactly your sit-down-and-be-safe kind of guy. I bumped my head. So what? It's not like I'm going to be any different than I was before the accident.

Jason

June 17

This is bull. I can't write worth crap. Everybody knows that. I'm a loser. Your basic reject.

Mr. B got to thinking. His first mistake.

Mistake #2: Crazy guy asked me to add thoughts to my drawings. Says I'm here, anyway. Might as well draw something for Logan to remember his hospital stay.

Me? Forget the trip down memory lane. I almost lost my best friend.

Logan

Why can't they just leave me alone? All of them—the nurses, the doctors, the therapists. Everyone. I'm sick of people in my face. Sick of all the tests.

My shrink says I'm depressed. You think? One day, I'm fine. The next day, I can't even remember how to count to 10. I keep waiting for things to clear, but my brain's so fuzzy. I'm starting to wonder if I'll ever be the same.

Doc says I have a traumatic brain injury. TBI for short. Translation: It's like having a migraine, a hangover and the flu all at once. Meds don't help. I'm tired all the time. I can't concentrate, and every word gets stuck in head space.

I just want to be normal again.

Jason
June 18

Sirens haunt me.

I stand over Logan's body. Terrified. The guys in the ambulance fight to keep him alive.

Rewind 10 minutes. Logan's trailer. Playing Xbox.

"Hungry?" Logan sniffed his armpits and grabbed a shirt on the floor.

I cursed when my guy got blown up.

"Ha, ha." Logan laughed. "I'm still top dog."

"Maybe. But yo mama's so ugly, Goldfish crackers don't smile back."

Logan threw a pillow, but I ducked.

"And yo mama's so stupid, she tries to alphabetize M&M's."

Our slam fest continued to the Quick Shop. Then we headed to the pool to see Jessie.

"You got it bad, Romeo," I harassed Logan. Jess is one of the guys. She knows her way under a hood 'cause her uncle's into demo cars.

"Shut up." Logan cursed. He fell hard the day Jess showed up in a hot pink bikini.

I slowed at the intersection, but Logan sped past me. He didn't see the blue pickup.

A horn blared. Tires squealed. Logan flew from his bike and smacked the asphalt. Blood pooled around his long black hair.

It happened so fast. I couldn't even warn Logan.

I was too slow.

Like always.

Logan

Doc says something, but I only pick out two words. Brain and engine.

My mind wanders to the '74 Nova me and my dad bought for a couple hundred bucks. The body's in pretty good shape, but the engine's messed up. Just like me.

She'll be one sweet ride after me and my dad overhaul the transmission and rebuild the engine. I want to paint her candy apple red and put new speakers in the back, but first comes the engine. Nothing works. A piston head is cracked, the spark plugs are shot and she needs a new carburetor. But now, everything has to wait, so the Nova sits outside rusting.

That's how I feel. Like I'm sitting in a hospital rusting. I can't do anything because it's all connected to a bad engine. My brain won't work, so everything—from talking to walking—is messed up. I lie in a hospital bed wondering if my brain can be rebuilt. It's like my eight-cylinder got knocked in half.

Jason
June 21

Someone nudges my shoulder. "Wake up, buddy."

I open an eye. The night nurse stares at me. I swipe at my mouth, hoping I didn't drool.

"It's time to go home."

I sit up. Logan is snoring in the hospital bed.

"You know you're not supposed to be here past visiting hours."

I shrug. Since when do I care about rules?

She smiles. "Logan's lucky to have a friend like you."

"So let me stay."

The nurse shakes her head. "Sorry. I can't."

I want to argue, but she's the nice nurse. Not the old witch I call Bedpan.

I grab my skateboard. The parking lot is deserted except for the night staff. It's not fair. I go home to sleep, but Logan's stuck in the hospital.

Alone.

Will he ever wake up from the nightmare called his life?

Logan

Cart wheels squeak. The smell of plastic food makes me gag. I open my eyes and push the tray away.

"You gotta eat," the girl says. Her blond hair is pulled back in a ponytail. She looks like she's in high school.

I shake my head. I'm not eating this crap. The tubes are gone. I want real food—a Whopper and fries. Or Jalapeno Cheetos and a Red Bull. Not hospital food.

The girl peels back the aluminum foil on my apple juice and sticks a straw into the cup. She might as well tie a bib around my neck. I feel like a freakin' baby.

I grab the juice, and it splashes all over my food. I pick up a soggy roll and throw it. I aim for the trashcan, but hit the girl instead.

She gets mad. I tune her out—which is easy since most of her words roll right off me without meaning.

The dimple on her cheek shows. "You're cute," I say. She gives me this look I don't understand, then leaves the room. End of conversation.

People say I'm impulsive because of my brain injury. Maybe I'm hard to understand, but try explaining girls. They're impossible to figure out.

"Samson's dead."

Logan looks up from his hospital bed, his face blank.

"Samson. The crawdad." We caught him down at the canal in May, but I don't explain. I don't give Logan details on Samson's escape or the awful stench, either. The hospital people said to use short sentences. One or two words.

"Samson?" Logan repeats.

I grab the picture dictionary his therapist uses. No crawdad pictures, so I point to a lizard. "Samson's dead."

"Dead?"

I nod. Logan's like a 3 year old, and I'm the dumb one. I fail classes because I'm stupid. Logan just doesn't do the work.

"Samson!" Logan pounds his fists against the bedrail like a little kid. He won't quit, so I call for help.

The nurses say Logan's outburst won't be the first. Something about the front part of the brain. Doc calls it the "oops" control. That's why Logan acts like a toddler. Or a drunkard.

Now Logan's asleep. Everything makes his brain tired. So he naps a lot. Just like a baby.

The hum of the machines gets on my nerves. I don't even know my best friend anymore.

Logan

My mind is a carnival of horrors. Fragments of thought and distorted memories leave me confused. Dazed. Trapped.

I miss ordinary things. Everyday things.

Wrestling with my kid brother.

Standing in the shower.

Dressing myself.

Eating pancakes on Saturday morning.

Walking down the block.

Lying in the grass.

Getting air on my skateboard.

Fighting with my sister.

Sleeping in.

Messing around with Jason.

My life.

This place adds to my madness. Disinfectant. Sponge baths. People in white jackets. Ugly plaster walls tighten around me, squeezing me in a vice of cinderblock and drywall.

The pressure crushes me, slowly killing me.

I'm dying.

Jason
June 24

"Moving day," the nurse I call Bedpan tells Logan. Her frown makes her look constipated.

I light up. "Logan gets to go home?"

Bedpan shakes her head. "Rehab. He's moving to a new facility. Logan's stable now, so he's got a lot to relearn. The closest hospital's in Lincoln."

"What?" This summer bites. "That's two hours away."

"Doctor's orders."

I want to rip her stethoscope in half, but I crank up the bass instead. Bedpan can't understand. The witch doesn't have friends.

She shuts off the power. "You need to leave."

I storm out of the room and find a vending machine. It's war now.

Bedpan is gone when I return with a Mountain Dew and a Baby Ruth.

"Watch this." I grab a real bedpan and empty the yellow fizz into the plastic pan. The chocolate looks like crap. Logan—the king of practical jokes—doesn't even crack a smile. Letting a bull snake loose in the cafeteria made him famous.

I push the call button.

Bedpan sticks her head in the door.

"Full." I point to the pan.

Bedpan dumps the contents into the toilet, then folds her arms across her chest. "Urine doesn't bubble. Next time use apple juice."

I bust out laughing. Logan is clueless.

"Leave." She points to the door.

I duck to avoid Bedpan.

She's just mean enough to give me a shot.

Logan

Rehab is hell. I'm all alone and two hours from home. I miss Jason's ugly mug. The dude's more faithful than a dog. He even slept at the hospital until the nurses kicked him out. Maybe Jason can hitch a ride when my parents rotate weekends to come visit me.

"Name the days of the week in order," the speech lady says real slow like I'm some retard. Her lipstick is faded, so a red line rings dry lips.

I squeeze my eyes shut. It helps to block out other noises— the tap of her pen against the clipboard, the scratch of a beetle's wings across the linoleum. If only I could flatten myself and slide under the crack of the door. Escape this prison.

"Sun—day." My voice sounds raspy, different than before. One more thing the accident changed. "Thurs—day." I let out a breath and rub my temples. "Tues—day."

"What comes next?" The speech lady looks down at her paperwork. She doesn't get it. The questions are too simple. I'm not some special ed case.

"Fri—day." I force myself to concentrate. "Mon—day."

She scribbles something and looks up at me.

My head throbs. I'm so tired.

"You worked hard today, Logan." She pats my hand and rises to leave. "More this afternoon."

I want to scream. My life's a freakin' schedule.

Jason

June 26

Logan

"Ughhh." I throw the stupid pincher tool across the floor. I can't do it.

"Deep breath," the occupational therapist says—OT for short. His cornrows shake when he bends to retrieve the tool. The dude looks like he could bench press a bus. Lucky him. He gets to hang out with a pasty white kid who can't even drop a beanbag in a stupid bucket.

Squeeze handle, grab beanbag, drop in bucket. It looks so easy. No big deal. Except I keep missing the bucket.

"Let's go outside," the OT says.

I don't think he's serious. I can barely fart if it's not on the schedule.

"Come on." He wheels me to the door.

"Really?" My voice squeaks, and he laughs. We wheel down the hall, past others like me. The young vet I met who lost a leg. A girl who told me she got thrown from her horse. A guy who looks like my grandpa after he had his stroke.

The OT opens the door, and sunlight burns my eyes. I'm an albino in a hospital gown.

"It's hotter than blazes." He wipes his forehead.

Maybe, but I gulp the fresh air like a starving man. Real air mixed with dog crap and cut grass. Not hospital oxygen sterilized to poorly disguise waste and vomit.

"Wanna sit over there?" He wheels me to a garden area on the hospital grounds. A man sits with his two boys eating McDonald's. I drool over the chicken nuggets.

"You mind?" The OT taps a pack of cigarettes against his hand.

I'd ask for a drag, but being outside is intoxicating enough.

"Our secret." He winks and blows smoke from the side of his mouth. "Everyone needs a break, huh?"

Yeah. Like a break from my life.

A '67 Camaro cruises through the parking lot, the subwoofers thumping. I imagine me behind the wheel with Jessie next to me.

"Sweet ride," the OT says.

My fantasy pops when one of the kids yells, "Heads up!" His bouncy ball lands in my lap.

The kid holds out his arms to catch the ball. When I finally grasp it, I miss the kid completely. The ball falls short. Way short.

I'm such a loser. Jessie will never want me.

"Patience, my friend." The OT knocks my shoulder. "You'll be making slam dunks in no time."

Whatever. I curse. I hate liars.

Jason

July 1

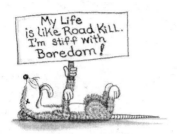

Logan has to be bored. I'm going postal.

Sometimes I hang out at his trailer, even though Logan's not there. It beats mine.

Today me and his younger brother are messing around when I hear the microwave door slam shut.

"Electricity's off," his mom yells to his dad. "Did you pay the bill?"

"I lost my job."

"You what?"

Silence. I peek around the corner. Logan's dad doesn't move from the recliner—just like when Logan was in the coma, and he sat beside the hospital bed for hours.

"They can't do that!" she screams. "We'll sue."

"We can't," Logan's dad mutters.

"Why not?" Her eyes flash. "There's that sick child law or whatever it's called."

"We can't." He hits the remote, but the television doesn't work. "I didn't show up for two weeks."

Logan's mom swears.

"My kid's stuck in a hospital, and I can't fix it. What good am I?"

I've never seen Logan's dad look so defeated. It scares me more than the fighting.

I got a rat once from the pet store. Beady eyes peered into mine as it ran around the wheel in the cage. The squeak of the metal in the middle of the night finally drove my mom mad, and I had to get rid of Goliath.

Now I'm stuck spinning on a rehab wheel. There's rehab, followed by rehab, followed by more rehab. Physical therapy, speech therapy, occupational therapy, nap. The afternoon repeats with a twist. Speech, OT, PT, bedtime. When I forget which rehab comes next—which happens a lot—there's a schedule on my wall for me, the human lab rat. Words don't mean much, so there's pictures—unless I forget those, too. Then the therapists come after me, and I keep spinning.

Spinning.

Spinning.

Spinning on my stupid wheel.

Jason

July 2

My old man is dead drunk when I hear a knock. Mr. B waits at the door. Our trailer's trashed. Grandma refuses to clean after 30 years as a hotel maid. She moved in after Mom left so the old man can truck.

"Do you have a laptop?" Mr. B asks.

"The screen's busted."

"I gotta show you something. Can you come to the school?"

I frown.

"No pop quizzes." He laughs and crosses his chest. "I promise."

Talk about creepy—a deserted school in the summer. Mr. B unlocks the building, and we walk toward the science labs. I peer into the glossy eyes of a rattlesnake floating in formaldehyde.

"Boo," Mr. B hisses, and I jump.

"Very funny."

Mr. B hands me a plastic model of a brain. "Here, hold this. I've been doing some research."

I don't know how to hold the brain, so I grip it like a football.

"Real brain tissue's soft enough to cut with a Popsicle stick." Mr. B powers up the computer and gets online. "Like JELL-O or tofu. Amazing considering everything our brains do."

Mental picture: the fake brains at last year's haunted house.

"Look at this." A diagram fills the screen. It's an inside peek at someone's head.

I hold up the brain model and compare it with the picture on the screen.

"Fluid normally cushions the brain." Mr. B points to the area between the brain and the skull. "But notice what happens during a concussion."

I lean closer, and he clicks the mouse. The head takes a hit.

Think crash test dummy in a wreck. The brain ricochets off the skull. It hurts just looking at the impact. Especially when I imagine Logan smashing into the asphalt.

Mr. B turns away from the computer. He nods toward an empty glass case in the corner. "Remember the ant tunnels?"

Yeah. Watching them was hypnotic—way better than homework.

"Imagine shaking an ant farm."

"The tunnels would be a mess. Like an Etch A Sketch when you destroy the picture."

"Exactly. The same thing happened to Logan," Mr. B says. "His network of connections got shaken. Now he's got to rebuild those pathways. It takes a lot of work and repetition for everyday tasks to become habit again."

Ants might be small, but they weren't lazy. Or stupid. Neither was Logan.

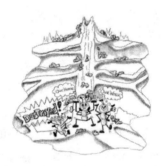

"We're on autopilot most of the time," Mr. B explains. "We walk to class or make a sandwich. We don't have to concentrate."

Except Logan. That's why he has trouble doing the simple things. Everyday things.

Mr. B ends the biology lesson. "Does that help clear things up?"

I nod. It's a lot to take in. "Thanks, Mr. B."

"My nephews call me PB." He locks up the lab. "Like peanut butter. Peter's my first name."

The nickname fits. The guy kinda sticks to you—even if he is a teacher.

Logan

"You're getting stronger," the PT says. My wheelchair sits empty in the corner.

I take a few steps and lose my balance. Just hand me a diaper. I'm more helpless than a baby.

"Easy." The PT reaches out for my arm, and I pull away.

My head feels like it could split in half.

"Ten steps," he says. "Then you can go to rec."

I bite down too hard. The sour taste of blood fills my mouth. Step with the right foot, follow with the left.

"There you go," the PT says. The dude could put on a skirt and grab some pompoms. He's worse than a freakin' cheerleader.

I'm winded when I touch the bars 30 feet away. It's the first time I make it.

"Awesome, Logan." The PT slaps me on the back.

I refuse to get all gushy, but I can't hide my smile.

"Keep it up, and you'll be outta this wheelchair before you go home."

My eyes bug out. It's been a long time since I heard good news.

PB's playing dumb. Who else could've left the mystery gas card for Logan's parents?

Logan's going to flip. He hasn't had a single guest since he moved to rehab almost two weeks ago. His dad can't find another job, and the bills are piling up. A road trip was out of the question until PB's gift.

Guess who gets to tag along?

Me.

Logan

"Jason?" I squeak like a stupid toy when he walks into my room.

"Surprised?" He grins. "Your dad's grabbing lunch, so he dropped me off."

It's so good to see the little punk.

"Happy Fourth." Jason pulls out a pack of Black Cats from a paper bag.

Have I been stuck in rehab that long? Every day blurs into the next.

Jason raises an eyebrow. "Can you say fun?"

Me and Jason live for the Fourth of July. Blowing up things is our favorite pastime. Watermelons, Barbie dolls, plastic cars—we blow it all up. The dumbest thing we ever tried was an empty paint can. The metal exploded into a hundred pieces of shrapnel. I almost lost an eye.

"Two words." Jason laughs.

I stare at him, letting my brain catch up.

"Water bomb."

Jason goes into some story, but I'm lost by the end of the first sentence. My blank expression finally makes him stop. "You don't remember, do you?"

I shake my head. Remembering is hard. Doc says my memory's like Swiss cheese. Lots of holes.

Jason gets up, and I think he's going to leave. I don't blame him. His best friend died the day of the accident.

Instead, Jason pushes my wheelchair to the bed. "Get in."

"What?" I say. Most people talk louder when I don't understand, but Jason doesn't. He knows I'm not deaf. I just have trouble understanding things. At least that's what they tell me.

30

"Get in." Jason motions to the chair beside my bed as he sets the brake.

I shake my head, but Jason won't accept no for an answer.

I stare at my wheelchair. I hate the thing, but I need it until I can walk again. Transferring from bed to chair is hard. No matter how many times I've practiced.

I exhale. I can do this.

Jason is patient. "You okay?"

The wheelchair taunts me. Jason looks like he wants to give me a hand, but he doesn't, and I'm glad. A guy can only take so much help.

My breathing is heavy when I finally make it.

"Party time." Jason pushes me down the hall. No one stops him. The staff is short for the holiday.

Me and Jason got in-school suspension for ditching school once. A memory I actually remember. The ex-Marine in charge chewed Red Man and smelled like the boys' locker room. It was the longest week of my life.

Jason wheels me past the empty waiting room. He checks the hall and pushes me into a single public restroom. The smell makes me gag.

"Sorry." Jason laughs. "We have to get creative."

He pulls out a box of water boomers and lights a punk.

"You're nuts."

"I learned from the master."

Bits of memory float to the surface. Mixing Tabasco sauce in a teacher's coffee. Egging the principal's car. Smoking in the locker room. All my ideas, I think.

Jason touches the punk to the fuse. The bittersweet smell of gunpowder fills the air. He tosses the water boomer into the toilet. It sinks a couple inches. *Pop.* Water shoots up. We bust out laughing.

Pop. Pop. Pop. Jason throws more bombs into the toilet. A droplet of water splashes onto my face, but I don't care. I can't remember the last time I had so much fun.

Jason hands me a bomb. "Go ahead." He lights the fuse. Sparks nip my skin when I hesitate.

"Throw it!" Jason shrieks like a girl.

I arch my hand, but my aim is off. The water bomb falls onto the floor.

Boom. The bomb explodes. Black powder smears the wallpaper.

Someone pounds on the door.

"Quick." Jason flushes the evidence down the toilet. Wet paper floats to the surface.

"Is everything okay in there?" a voice calls out. My heart thumps against my chest.

Jason swears. He dips his hand into the toilet and swipes up the last of the soggy bombs. He stuffs them into his pocket and pushes me out the door like nothing happened.

A nurse narrows her eyes. The smell is going to give us away.

"Sorry," Jason mutters. "His wheelchair got stuck."

She frowns, but we don't stick around. I never knew my chair could go so fast.

Jason

July 14

Hershey licks PB to death when he pulls up on his bike outside our trailer. The dude's crazy about biking. Just like I used to be.

"What's that?" PB points to my sketchbook. Too late to hide it.

"Nothing," I lie. I spend hours with my sketchbook.

"Can I look?" PB asks.

Logan's the only one who's seen my stuff.

"I swear I won't laugh."

PB flips through the pages. He stops at my eagle cartoons from the canal.

My face gets hot.

"You drew these?"

PB is impressed, but I shrug off the attention. In the winter, eagles hang out near the power plant because the turbines on the canal stun the fish. It's like fast food for birds. A kiddie meal without the stupid toy.

I don't talk to adults, but PB's different. The girls at school revolted when he married the music teacher last year. They say he's hot, like the actor in that vampire movie. Me? I'm too skinny and too white. At least I got my mom's green eyes.

33

"Want to go for a ride?"

"On bikes?" I stopped riding after the accident.

"We'll take it real slow."

I'm quiet.

"You can do it." PB heads to the shed. "Is this where you keep your bike?"

I exhale.

"Don't let fear stop you."

I get up the nerve to straddle the seat on my Haro, but my hands are shaking.

"Let's start with the neighborhood."

I squeeze my eyes shut and see Logan lying in his blood.

"You okay?" The bike wobbles until I get my legs. PB cheers like a wild man. He even convinces me to bike to McDonald's for lunch.

Back home, I'm practically soaring. Then the old man pulls up in his rig and rips into me for not mowing. He fails to notice my bike.

Even worse—the man doesn't have a clue I haven't ridden for a month.

Logan

I scratch a mark for every day at rehab, like a survivor on a deserted island. Instead of tree bark, I scribble under the toilet paper in the bathroom. It's almost symbolic considering how my life stinks.

I mark another day when I hear the door open.

"Good morning," the OT calls out. I can't even take a dump without the whole world knowing. I flush the toilet in greeting.

"Where's Tyrone?" I frown when I see a woman.

"Sick." She's way too perky. "Ready to work?"

I woke up in a foul mood, and she's not helping. Doc calls them my black moods. Comes with brain injuries.

"We're going to play a little game." She pouts when I don't get excited.

The OT puts several objects on the table. "Is the bouncy ball green?"

I hate these stupid questions.

"Is the ball bigger than the slinky?"

Who cares?

"Logan," she repeats. "Is the ball bigger than the slinky?"

A memory comes to the surface. My brother left a slinky on the steps when we were kids. I tripped and got five stitches.

"You gotta concentrate." Her voice is distant.

I let out a puff of air. "Slinky."

"Now put the green ball into the box."

I follow the directions, but that's not enough. She adds another step. "Take the green ball out of the box, add the slinky and close the lid."

I grab the slinky, but forget what's next.

The OT repeats the sequence, this time slower.

I get mad and throw the box on the floor.

35

"Let's try something else." Ms. Perky picks up the box.

I'm supposed to make a pattern with four different shapes. Circle, square, oval, rectangle. Repeat. Easy, except I keep messing up.

I curse. Do this. Do that. Work harder. Concentrate.

I can't. Don't they get it? My brain doesn't work.

Jason
July 20

"I'm afraid to see him," Jess admits to me. We're at the demo derby watching her uncle cruise around in his sweet '68 Pontiac Bonneville. Logan's always with us, so it's weird without him.

Dust rises in a cloud as cars collide. The noise makes it hard to talk, but that doesn't stop Jess.

"I'm an awful person, huh?" She wrinkles her nose—something Logan would think is cute. "I should visit Logan at the rehab hospital."

I don't know how to explain the new Logan.

"He's different."

Jess has seen pictures on Facebook. "Is his hair growing back?"

"A little. He looks like a new recruit for the Army."

The crowd jumps to its feet. We cheer as Jess' uncle slams into an '89 Chevy Caprice station wagon. The back crumples. Her uncle shows no mercy.

"I can't even imagine what Logan's going through," Jess says. "One day, he's normal. The next day, he can't even remember the alphabet."

I watch the action in the ring. The station wagon isn't moving, and the driver's cussing up a storm.

Jess points to the Chevy. "You think that's how Logan feels?"

I'm not sure what Jess means.

"Stuck," she says.

I follow her gaze. The station wagon isn't going anywhere.

Rehab is Logan's only hope—no matter how much he hates it. Otherwise he won't be any better off than the Chevy Caprice. Logan will be stuck his whole life.

"It's natural to be frustrated," the shrink says. Her hair is too orange, a dye job gone bad. "Let's talk about those feelings."

Touchy-feely crap isn't going to change anything.

"Logan?"

I stare out the window. I should just jump. Get it over with now.

"I'm gonna assume you're listening." She pulls something from her desk drawer. "Even if you don't want to talk."

A plastic gun. Great, the woman spends too much time with mental people.

"It's a toy." It squeaks when she squeezes.

"Things are going to frustrate you," the shrink explains. "But you can't give up. You have to retrain your brain."

My head hurts.

"You need some secret weapons."

Give me a real gun, and I'll let out some frustration.

"The toy gun is a reminder—like a string around your finger. Stick it in your pocket for the hard days when you forget."

Forget what? That I had a bike accident? That I can't do anything? If only I could forget. "Are we done yet?"

She taps a manicured fingernail against the desk. "When you get frustrated, pull out your secret weapon."

I point the toy at her face and cock the trigger. *Bam.*

She doesn't even react. "What's one thing that made you mad today?"

"Therapy."

Again—no reaction. "Something else that angered you?"

"The toothpaste." I chucked it into the toilet when I couldn't squeeze it on my brush.

"How many chances did you give it?"

"One." This is a waste of time.

"Secret weapon #1." She grins like an idiot. "Give everything three chances."

"So three strikes, you're out?"

The shrink stands to leave. "Third time's also a charm."

Jason

July 28

Riding a bike is way easier. PB says courage isn't the absence of fear. It's acting in spite of it. That's what the guy who wrote *Tom Sawyer* said, anyway.

Maybe. But I'm not the one who got messed up in the accident. Logan doesn't talk about it, but I know he's afraid. Will he ever be normal? Will he ever ride again? Or will the fear haunt him? Like a dragon ready to scorch his butt.

Logan

"Good news." The therapist types some notes into my chart.

I raise my eyebrows. "No more wheelchair?"

His eyes smile behind wire-rimmed glasses. "You're clear."

"Yes!" I pump my arm in victory.

"No skateboard stunts—yet." The therapist knows my daredevil reputation. "And then you better be wearing a helmet."

I feel like doing cartwheels, except I trip over my feet on my way out the door. My chin smacks a treadmill. Blood drips all over my shirt.

"Like I said." He shakes his head, and a nurse cleans me up. "Helmet."

I frown.

"It's better than the alternative." The therapist gives me a long warning look. "You could wind up in the chair again."

I curse. I'd rather be in a body cast.

Jason

August 1

I see PB's bike parked outside the school when I'm out riding around, so I tap on his window. He meets me at the back door dressed in paint clothes. "Your helmet's no good if it's not strapped."

I ignore him. "Nice pants."

A custodian walks by with a load of trash. "Got some help painting?"

PB eyes me. "Hope so. Jason's an artist."

I give a humph. I'm not used to compliments. "What're you doing?"

"Trying to paint the solar system. Wanna see?"

I follow PB. Black paint covers a wall in his classroom.

"I can barely draw stick people." He laughs. "Wanna help me with the planets?"

It's not like I have anything better to do. I grab a brush and step across the drop cloth. Splattered paint would make a great night sky.

Two hours later, me and PB are at Pizza Hut. My pay for helping out.

He orders a large pizza. "Thanks for your help."

I think about the finished mural back at school. "It looks good."

PB blows his straw wrapper at me. "So when does Logan come home?"

"Two days." I can't wait.

"You know it's gonna be different, right?"

I shrug. At least Logan won't be two hours away.

PB gets quiet. He draws something on a napkin.

I tease him about the kiddie crayon.

"What do you see?" PB asks.

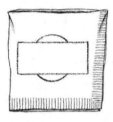

I may be stupid, but I know my shapes.

"Humor me," PB says. "Tell me what you see."

"A circle behind a rectangle." Our pizza comes, so I dig in.

PB draws in dotted lines to form two circles. "How many?"

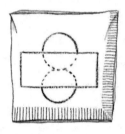

I shake my head and speak with a mouthful. "Not two. One circle." I redraw the rectangle and dotted lines to show him what I'd pictured in my mind.

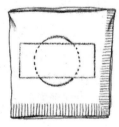

"Exactly." PB taps my picture. "We don't see two circles because our brains complete the picture."

Even I know he's talking about Logan. "Unless you have a brain injury."

44

PB nods. "I'm just as thrilled as you that Logan gets to come home. But things aren't going to be the same." He reaches across the table and pats my shoulder. "Try to remember that on the hard days."

The hard days? Logan's coming home. For once things are looking up.

Logan

"Logan!" My kid sister Brianna takes a flying leap into my hospital bed.

"Ugh." I don't move quick enough to avoid the knee to my groin. I'm too happy to get mad. Today I get out of this miserable hole.

Something between a tornado and a tsunami overtakes my room. My parents and Dylan follow Brianna.

"Turn it down," Dad barks at Dylan. Music thumps through his earphones.

"Point me to the bathroom." Mom raises her 64-ounce fountain drink. "Or it's not going to be pretty."

I sit up, trying to make sense of everything.

My dad talks about the drive to Lincoln. I nod like I understand.

Brianna interrupts, but her words are so fast, I don't catch much. Something about a trampoline.

"The neighbors just bought one." Mom comes out of the bathroom. The light catches the silver bead in her tongue.

I'm still trying to picture the neighbors when Brianna starts in about something else.

Dylan pushes the call button for the nurses. "This place sucks. The remote don't even work."

"Moron." Brianna grabs the real remote, and sounds blast from the TV.

Dylan makes a face, and the two fight. I cover my ears. The noise is like a jackhammer to my head.

"You called?" A nurse pushes open the door.

No one hears her.

"You okay?" the nurse asks me. Her perfume is too strong, I want to gag.

"I'm fine," I lie. I don't want anything to spoil the day.

Dylan flips through the channels too fast. Images burn on my mind. A deodorant commercial. A game show host. An alligator submerged in swampy water. I close my eyes.

Sounds bounce through my head like ping pong balls. Snatches of conversation mix with the chaos.

My sister grabs the leftover cookie on my tray and knocks over the juice I didn't finish. Liquid sprays my dad. He explodes.

My mom lights a cigarette. She stopped smoking a month before my accident. I remember because we celebrated at DQ. Now she smokes more than before.

I feel like I could puke.

The nurse jumps in like a drill sergeant. She sends Dylan and Brianna out of the room and makes my mom put out her cigarette. She turns to a mountain of paperwork and hands the first form to my parents.

My dad grunts. Mom drags her chair closer.

"Logan has come a long way," the nurse says.

Papers shuffle between my parents. I let my head roll back. I'm so tired.

Most of what the nurse says makes no sense. Post-concussion syndrome. Levels of cognitive functioning. Aphasia. The words blow up around me like land mines.

Dylan and Brianna are back. Brianna pulls a long string of bubble gum from her mouth and twists it around her finger. "This is boring."

Dylan calls her something, and Brianna wails. "Mom!"

The vein at my dad's temple throbs.

The nurse pauses and takes a deep breath. "Logan will need a lot of support."

"More therapy?" my dad interrupts. "I can't pay the bills we got now."

"Expect a lot of anger and irritability." The nurse looks at me. "Simple things are hard for Logan, so he gets frustrated easily."

"Mom!" Brianna whines when Dylan takes the remote. It's so loud.

My dad jumps from his seat. Dylan retreats to the corner, while Brianna starts to cry. Mom tries to light another cigarette until the nurse stops her.

"Logan's life changed 180 degrees." The nurse doesn't hide her irritation.

"Like mine didn't?" Dad snaps.

"This is a difficult time." She dares to confront my dad.

"Difficult?" He gets in her face. "I got creditors calling, bills piling to the ceiling and no job."

"I understand." The nurse backs up. "The family counselor will be here shortly."

"I don't need any more family shrink sessions!" my dad screams. "I need a job. Not a stinking head doctor." He storms out of the room, swearing all the way down the hall.

I clutch my head. It hurts so bad. What if going home turns into a nightmare?

Jason

August 3

"Think he'll be surprised?" Jess looks over our decorating attempt. She's dressed in a mini-skirt and a denim jacket—not her usual jeans and t-shirt. Balloons and streamers fill Logan's trailer.

"Looks good, guys." PB sets a cake from the bakery on the table.

I try to nab some frosting, and he slaps my hand.

"Logan should be here any minute," PB says.

We go outside, and sure enough, the van pulls around the corner. PB grabs his welcome sign and starts cheering. Me and Jess join in. My best friend is finally home.

Logan's dad doesn't honk in celebration. The van pulls in the driveway, and his mom tosses a cigarette from the window. "Sorry, guys. No party today. Logan needs to rest."

Me and Jess look at PB. "Long trip?" he asks.

She reeks of smoke. "I went through a box of cigarettes. And that was just the first 30 miles."

Dylan slides open the back door. Logan's eyes are puffy. I've never seen him cry.

"Welcome home," I say.

Logan doesn't even crack a smile. He grips his head and stumbles to the door. A lone balloon escapes. So much for a happy homecoming.

Logan

Jason knocks on my bedroom door, but I ignore him.

"Here's some breakfast." He sets a tray down.

I pull the blankets to my chin and turn to the wall. "Go away."

I don't want to leave my room.

Ever.

Jason

August 12

I'm taking Logan hostage. It's been a week, and he refuses to leave his trailer. He loves the fair—we go every year—so I figure I'll surprise him. My grandma drops us off at the fairgrounds.

We're not even there five minutes, and I know I've made a mistake. The flashing lights bother Logan. His face is twisted in pain.

I decide to steer Logan away from the rides and toward the games.

Bad idea. Logan throws a fit at the shooting gallery when a kid wins a stuffed alien. Good thing the guns aren't real. He might hurt someone.

I distract Logan with a big lollipop.

"I want that." He eyes a huge Tasmanian devil at the basketball hoops.

It's pointless to argue, even though Logan misses every shot.

"My baby sister can throw better than that." A kid laughs, and Logan swears like a madman.

The kid flips him off.

I pull Logan away before he strangles the brat. "Let's eat something."

The menu overwhelms Logan. He has that deer-in-the-headlights look, so I give him two choices. "Funnel cake or cotton candy?"

Logan stands there with a dead battery for a brain.

The line grows behind us.

"People are waiting, kid," the lady at the counter snaps. "What'd you want?"

Funnel cake sounds good, but I don't want a scene. "Let's get out of here."

Logan follows me like a zombie.

"It's gonna be okay," I mumble. But I don't believe my lies.

Logan

Being home's rough, but at least I don't have to eat hospital food.

My little sister's at the kitchen table when I open the frig. "Can you help me?" Brianna holds up a princess coloring book.

I forget about the food. We sit at the table and color.

"You don't do it like Mommy," Brianna says. "She stays in the lines."

I dig the marker into the page, and it rips.

"Look what you did." Brianna calls me stupid and huffs out of the room.

My stomach grumbles, and I remember I'm hungry. I can't find any chips, so I head to the Quick Shop.

I pass the skate park, and skaters swarm me.

"Dude, where's your board?" Someone hands me a skateboard. I run my fingers over the grip tape. It's been a long time. Too long.

"You still king of the board?"

I curse and jump on the board. It wobbles underneath me.

"You okay, man?"

I grit my teeth. My legs are spaghetti. I throw out my arms to catch my balance.

Someone laughs.

I growl, and the crowd backs away. I kick the board, and it bangs against the pavement.

"Dude, that's my new board!" Hands grab my shirt and throw me down. My head hits the grass. My world goes black.

A voice finally breaks the fog.

I blink. I don't know how long I've been out. My head kills.

"What happened?" Jason and Jessie stand over me.

I sit up and almost pass out.

"You okay?" Jessie leans over me.

I think I'm seeing stars. "You smell nice."

"Did someone jump you?" Jason asks.

I can't remember.

Jason and Jessie look at each other. "We need to get you home," Jason says.

Now I'm mad. "I'm not a baby." I stumble to my feet, and Jessie tries to help.

"Leave me alone." I yank my arm away and stomp off.

"Doc said he could get mean," Jason tells Jessie.

"I can hear you," I call back.

"Then don't push us away." Jason jogs up to me. "We have to tell your parents you blacked out."

"You're not my babysitter." I scowl. My stomach grumbles. That's when I remember I never made it to the Quick Shop. I hate my brain.

Jason

August 15

It's midnight, and I'm at Logan's with Hershey. The details are a little fuzzy, but my grandma's dead. I found her on the kitchen floor after school, black coffee pooled around her grey hair. Shattered pieces of porcelain littered the linoleum.

I can't sleep. The old man says I'm going to Tennessee to live with my uncle. He's stoned out worse than the old man.

I can't leave. Not when Logan needs me. Life sucks.

"She's really dead." Jason's words echo in the still morning air. We're at the river. Away from the trailer park. "My grandma's gone."

A hawk soars above us, and I watch its reflection on the surface of the river.

Jason points to my fishing line. "Hey, you got something."

I'm too slow. The fish escapes. I squish another worm. Casting my line is even more pathetic.

Jason pats Hershey's head. "It's weird at home with just me and the old man."

I remember when Jason's mom left. He wouldn't come out of his room for days.

"The old man says I gotta move."

"Move?" I repeat the word.

"To Tennessee."

"Tennessee?" I don't understand.

Jason untangles my fishing line. "Where my uncle lives."

Panic hits me. "You're leaving me?"

Jason breaks the line and reties my hook. "You got it stuck good."

I want to hit something. "It's not fair."

"Try convincing the old man." Jason hands me my pole.

I kick the dirt. Things are bad enough. My best friend can't move.

Jason
August 17

I stare at the blank page. Even sketching doesn't help me forget my life.

I flip through my sketches and stop. My fingers trace a face. My mom. Memory hits me. She's dancing. Country music fills my ears. Her long blond hair moves as she spins around our kitchen, and I watch from the doorway.

"Wanna dance, handsome?" Her German accent is thick. I'm so clumsy, but she's real patient teaching me step after step. It's the best day of my life.

I close my eyes and hear her sing a German lullaby. That's where she and the old man met. In Germany when he was stationed there with the Army.

I can't remember the words. Memory's weird that way. Like Logan's accident. It screwed up his life, and he can't even remember what happened.

Doing leg lifts bites, but I gotta do something or I'm going to explode. Jason can't leave me.

My dad walks into the room and grunts. We don't talk much anymore. Sweat rolls between my shoulder blades. I hate home therapy.

Dad pops the tab on a beer and hits the recliner. The electricity's back, but not cable, so he tunes out with public television. The trailer's a mess.

Maybe I can surprise Mom with supper. She's so tired all the time.

I get out Hamburger Helper. The pictures on the box look so easy, but they don't break down the steps enough.

An hour later, the noodles are crunchy, the hamburger's burnt and dirty dishes are scattered everywhere. Mom loses it. She and my dad get into a nasty fight.

It's my fault. Just like not having money for Dylan's birthday. If I didn't get banged up, Dad would still have his job and the bills would be paid.

Everything's falling apart. And I don't know how to fix it—just like the stupid Hamburger Helper.

Jason

August 19

I'm running away after the funeral. Last night I stashed my bike and bag behind the church. The old man will kill me, but I don't care. I almost lost Logan once. I won't lose him now.

Grandma looks different in the open casket. Not so hard. I want my sketchbook, but they'd send me farther than Tennessee for that. You just don't go around sketching dead people.

I ditch my funeral clothes and sneak off as soon as it's clear. I grab a Mountain Dew at the Quick Shop, and a faded picture falls out of my wallet. It's of Mom and the old man. He's in his desert camo.

I sit on the curb outside the store and remember the day the old man left for Iraq. I was 5 or 6. His hair was buzzed—not long and wild like now.

"Cheese!" The old man dipped my mom like they were dancing. I snapped the photo. They both glow.

War changed the old man. When he got back, the heat reminded him of the desert. Our trailer didn't have AC, so he'd grab a case of beer and disappear in his truck for hours. Then he and Mom would fight. No more wrestling on the floor with him. No playing ball. Nothing. The dad I knew was gone. That was the summer me and Logan sliced our fingers and pledged to be blood brothers for life.

"Who's in the picture?"

I jump. PB stands in front of me. His truck is parked at the gas pump.

"Didn't mean to scare you." He's still in his dress clothes. "You lit out so fast, I didn't have a chance to talk to you."

I can't even run away without messing up.

"He looks different." PB points at the picture. "Happy. Proud."

I jam the photo in my wallet. I don't want to talk.

"I know about Tennessee," he says. "I bet you'll miss Logan."

My jaw tightens. "I'm not going."

"I don't blame you. I wouldn't want to go, either."

I narrow my eyes. "So you gonna rat me out? Or let me run away?"

"Neither." PB meets my stare. "Maybe there are other options."

"Options?" I sneer. "My mom's gone, my grandma's dead and the old man trucks during the week. I'm not going into foster care."

PB gets this weird look.

"What?"

"Nothing."

"What?" I press.

"You wouldn't like it." PB shakes his head.

"Wouldn't like what?"

"Living with me and my wife during the week."

60

I almost laugh. "Live with you? A teacher?"

"I don't have teacher cooties. And we have a guest room in our apartment."

I frown. "Why do you care?"

PB gets a far-off look. "Maybe someone helped me once."

He doesn't say more, and I don't ask.

"I can talk to your dad if you want," PB offers. "I could use help tutoring Logan, anyway."

"You're tutoring Logan?"

"The teachers met last week. He's not ready to start back to school full-time."

I exhale. "The old man will never agree."

"Just let me ask."

It's pointless, but I don't argue. I'll be in Tennessee by the end of the week.

Logan

"Roll it like this." Dylan takes a newspaper from me. My brother's been doing my paper route since the accident.

I try to follow, but I end up with a wad of balled up paper. Broken rubber bands litter the floor.

"Tighten as you roll." Dylan snaps another rubber band in place. A pile grows beside him.

My head throbs. Before the accident, I could roll a hundred papers in 10 minutes, eyes closed. Fifteen when I had to use the rain bags.

Dylan tries to help, but I yank my paper away. Pages scatter everywhere. I kick them, cursing.

"What in the world?" Mom comes in. A cloud of newsprint floats around my head. "Time out," she says, but I'm too mad to pay attention.

"Logan." She puts her hands on my shoulders.

I'm breathing heavy.

"Time out. Fifteen minutes."

The shrink's idea—surprise, surprise. According to her, my fuse is too short. Blame something else on my brain injury.

I storm into my room and slam the door. I'm not a moron.

"I turned on the oven timer," my mom calls out.

I curse under my breath. Another one of Madame Shrink's ideas. She says I need that long for my emotions to calm down.

I hear the front door shut. Dylan's delivering my papers. Earning my money. I throw a shoe against my wall. Why is everything so hard?

Jason
August 20

The old man must've been drunk when PB called. He actually agreed to PB's idea. I don't have to move to Tennessee.

I run over to Logan's trailer. "Time to celebrate."

"Huh?" He's confused.

"Come on."

It takes Logan 10 minutes to tie his shoes. When we finally leave the trailer, I tell him about living with PB. It takes a while for things to sink in.

Twenty minutes later, we're at the drive-in movie theater. The big screen is showing its age, but we sneak in all the time. Logan's confused when I outline our attack.

"Now!" I push him out of the bushes. Logan trips, but the lady selling tickets doesn't see him. She's too busy helping a van full of kids.

"Come on!" I pull Logan up, and we run for the snack bar. I buy two Dr Peppers.

The big screen lights up the darkness, and we find a spot near some people on lawn chairs. Logan presses his hand against his temple.

"You okay?"

"Yeah," Logan lies. I know that look. A killer headache is coming on.

I glance at the movie and imagine the overload on Logan's brain. Flashes of light, moving pictures, loud sound. It's too much too fast.

I want to see the movie, but Logan's miserable. "Want to leave?"

Relief floods his face.

So much for celebrating.

Logan

I don't do libraries. And now I'm stuck here every afternoon for an hour.

PB takes out a stack of flashcards.

I'm not some stupid preschooler. I don't want a tutor. I want to go to school all day like every other normal kid—not just a couple classes in the mornings and leave after lunch. I even have to take naps to rest my brain.

PB holds out the first card. He meets me at the library at the end of his school day.

"What's this?" I'm supposed to name the object as quick as I can.

I cross my arms.

"I'll give you a hint." PB smiles. "Think zoo."

As in caged animal? Like me. I'm a prisoner to my own messed-up brain.

"Come on," PB says again. "Is it a monkey?"

I scowl. I'm not in the mood.

"Nod yes, or shake no." PB moves his head in demonstration.

I ignore him, but PB doesn't quit. "Elephant? Rhinoceros? Kangaroo?"

I hit the table. "Leave me alone."

PB puts the cards away. "Let's take a walk. Get some fresh air."

I shake my head.

PB pulls out a game of checkers. I won't play, so he stacks the checkers on top of each other in a tower. I stare at the clock. We sit like this—PB stacking checkers and me staring at the clock—for a long time. Finally, PB packs up.

"See you tomorrow," he says.

I curse under my breath.

"And the next day." PB speaks real slow. "And the next day. And the day after that."

I punch my backpack.

"You have a brain injury." PB looks right into my eyes. "Not a death sentence."

I turn away. I don't want to hear anymore.

"You can beat this." PB won't shut up. "Or it can beat you." He taps me on the shoulder when I won't look at him. "You decide."

Jason

August 22

"Wake up, Sleeping Beauty!" PB shakes me.

"Go away." I roll over.

Bright light burns my eyes. "Rise and shine. It's time to move out."

"What time is it?"

"Five o'clock."

"In the morning?" I squeak. Obviously my voice isn't up yet, either.

"Get up. We're biking."

I shove my pillow over my face. "You're insane."

"No, just in training." PB pulls off my covers and flashes a big grin. "You are, too, now that you live under my roof."

"Whoa," I protest. "I didn't sign up for boot camp." Tennessee's starting to look good.

"I'm biking on BRAN."

"Huh?" What's cereal got to do with anything?

PB laughs at my confusion. "Bike Ride Across Nebraska. B-R-A-N."

I sit up. "Isn't that like a couple hundred miles?"

"Almost 500." PB whistles to Hershey. "Get him, boy."

Dog slobber gets me out of bed. At least dogs are allowed at PB's apartment—and PB was cool with me bringing Hershey.

"Five minutes. Or you're biking in your underwear."

I pull on a black t-shirt. Biker Boy hands me a helmet, reflective vest and two water bottles. His wife, Laura, offers me a banana and granola bar. I don't do health food, but I'm too freakin' tired to argue.

"Have fun, boys." She kisses PB and heads for the gym.

I grunt. I want my bed.

PB has an extra road bike he lets me ride—an older Cannondale model. My Haro is great for riding around town or getting air on the dirt ramps, but not good for highway riding.

It's weird riding in the dark. PB's light moves up and down in front of me, like a bobber on a fish line. There's so many stars out in the open. It's quiet except for the whir of our spokes and the buzz of insects. Sometimes a train goes by, and the rickety *clack-clack* of metal against the track sounds for miles. We don't talk much.

My stomach roars when we ride into Odessa eight miles away. It's so small, there's not even a convenience store.

We get home in time to shower, eat and head to school.

"You could join the Army." PB grins. "You've already done more than most people do all day."

I curse under my breath.

Logan

I remember why I hate school—even if I am just here for a few hours. First day back, and I have a run-in with the pretty boys.

Austin sticks his head into the resource room. "Tough kid's hangin' with the retards now."

"At least Jason won't be alone," Mike snorts, and the two howl.

The teacher—Ms. J—chases them out.

I curse. Five minutes later, I think of a comeback. "At least I'm not ugly," I mutter.

The words sound stupid—even to me.

Jason

August 25

Lucky me. I'm on a training schedule. PB wants me to bike half centuries (50 miles) and centuries by spring. The guy's a lunatic.

Excuses don't work. Homework. Headache. Nothing.

We bike past Odessa to Elm Creek and turn south. I'm sweating like a dog. "Can we go home yet?"

PB pedals harder. I want to smack the guy.

"Wanna get wet?" He stops at the sandpits and kicks off his shoes.

I ditch my bike and peel off my shirt. A long rope hangs from a tree. I grab it and fly through the air. Talk about a rush.

PB lands a belly flop. I laugh, so he dunks me, and we get in a water fight. My shoes squish on the ride home.

"Glad you stuck it out today?" PB asks.

I shrug. It's too early to admit anything.

Logan

"Dude, you got something stuck in your teeth." Jason kicks me under the cafeteria table, but I don't connect. Jessie's headed toward us. Her long hair's highlighted from the summer sun.

"Teeth." Jason tosses me a napkin.

"Hey, Jason. Hi, Logan." Jessie stands in front of me. She's wearing make-up, and I can smell her perfume.

Jessie and Jason talk about her uncle's demolition car, but I can't keep up. I watch Jessie's lips—moistened with gloss—as they move, forming words that spin around my head.

"Kiss me." The words rush out of my mouth before I can stop them. Jessie turns red.

"I gotta go." She hurries off.

Jason thunks me in the head. "Smooth, Romeo."

"Ouch." I want to disappear. Now Jessie knows I'm a retard.

Jason
August 27

First weekend with the old man and he's drunk.

Hanging out at Logan's trailer isn't better. Dylan's angry. Brianna's sad. His mom's tired. And his dad doesn't move from the recliner.

It's not fair. The accident changed everything. And the police never found the hit-and-run driver.

Logan may never be the same. He talks so s---l---o---w. And he has to concentrate real hard for a two-word sentence.

I feel so helpless—and that's the worst.

Logan

PB reads a paragraph. I'm supposed to pick out the main idea, but my mind wanders. I stare at a knot in the wood on the desk. It looks like one of those trolls with the wild hair.

I hate this stupid cubicle. It's too small. We moved here because I'm too distracted out in the main library. Whatever.

A spider in the corner dangles from a silky thread. Long legs bend like a trapeze artist on a tightrope. The crowd goes silent. Will the spider fall?

"Logan?" PB's looking at me.

"Huh?" I blink.

"What did I just read about?"

I need a picture, some clue. My stomach grumbles. I say the first thing that comes to mind. "Pizza."

"You're guessing."

PB doesn't buy my innocent look.

"You need to concentrate." PB reads again.

Concentrate. If it were only that easy. Words float around my head like dust bunnies. Some land; most fly away.

Shark. Stingray. Swordfish. I cling to words as meaning takes shape.

PB raises his eyebrows. He's finished reading.

"The ocean," I answer.

"Close." PB gives me a hint. "Glass tank."

Fish dart through my head, then plunge into the dark places in my brain. PB waits for my answer. I can't remember.

"Aquarium," PB says.

I sink into my chair. He makes it seem so easy.

Jason
September 4

I'm living with Mr. Clean.
Make my bed.
Take out the trash.
Unload the dishwasher.
Vacuum.
Homework is bad enough. I feel like a freakin' Boy Scout.

Laura says I'm good for PB. No more dirty socks on the floor or empty pizza boxes on the coffee table. PB gets to be my role model.

Yeah for me.

"Dude, you gotta listen to this." Jason hands me the headphones at the music store in the mall. AC/DC booms through the speakers. He's old school when it comes to music. His old man got him hooked. It's the only thing they have in common.

Jason turns off the music.

I get mad. "What'd you do that for?"

Jason points to my head. He says I don't get clues from my body—like when a headache is coming on.

I punch the play button. "You're not my doctor."

"Fine." He backs off. A woman picks out some music next to me. One of her twins darts behind a display.

"Boo!" he screams.

The other boy jumps, and the display crashes down. CDs tumble to the ground.

"Stupid kids," I mutter.

The first one kicks me in the knee. I lunge after him, and he starts wailing. Jason grabs me before I can smack the kid. The mom calls for the manager.

"You need to leave," he tells me.

"What?" I curse. "It's the brat's fault."

Jason explains my brain injury.

"Looks normal to me," the manager says.

"That's the problem." Jason gets frustrated. "He's not."

We leave the store, both mad. "Dude, you just need a big bandage on your head."

Jason's right. At least then people would know something's wrong with me.

Jason

September 13

Sometimes I wish I could bike and sketch at the same time. We pass this abandoned café with a faded sign that reads *Oyster Stew on Special*. Something about it strikes me. I hate oysters, but it reminds me of chili and oyster stew on Christmas Eve—a family tradition that stopped when Mom left.

Another café, Grandma's Kitchen, makes my stomach grumble. I'm jealous of the farmers eating eggs and drinking coffee. I wonder if they notice the crazy early morning bikers. I can't believe it, but we finish 30 miles today. It's a miracle.

Logan

They're fighting again. My parents forget the walls are paper thin.

I cover my ears with my pillow. My shrink says we need more family counseling like when I was in rehab. Dad says talking won't change crap. Maybe he's right, but fighting's no better.

The door slams. Dad leaves to work on the Nova. Mom cries in the bedroom.

I'm the reason they fight. The stress is making us all crazy.

I go outside. "Want help?"

He grunts. "Hand me the crescent wrench."

The tool box is full. Which one's the wrench?

"I'm waiting." Dad's voice echoes from under the hood.

I grab the closest tool. "Here."

"Not the pliers."

My hands shake. I can hear the impatience in his voice.

"Wire cutters," my dad hisses when I mess up again.

I make one more guess.

"Never mind." Dad storms over to the tool box.

"Sorry," I mutter, but he's already under the hood.

I close my eyes, breathing in the dust and grease. Before the accident, my dad taught me how to change the oil and how to flush the radiator. Now, I can't even pump gas without a step-by-step picture. I'm so pathetic.

Dad hums along to the radio. A memory surfaces. The two of us, wrenches in hand, singing like rock stars.

I laugh, and it startles my dad. He bumps his head on the hood and curses.

"I thought you left," he growls.

I hang my head and let the door bang behind me.

Jason

September 24

The old man keeps drilling me about PB. What's Mr. Popularity really like? Do I still think he's cool now that I live with him?

"Why do you care?" I finally snap. "Are you jealous?"

He stomps off to the liquor store. And the rest of the weekend is just like every other one. Good old Pops drinks. And I disappear.

Sometimes I just wish I could hitchhike away from my life. Why didn't my mom take me with her?

"Ready for a challenge?" PB asks.

Now what? I just stumbled through naming a stack of cards.

"You can do it."

When I groan, PB points to the schedule for the day. The pictures taunt me. Three more tasks.

I close my eyes. I'm so tired.

"Time for some matching." PB spreads out a bunch of picture cards and words. He makes me go over everything a hundred times so maybe something will stick.

I pick up a word and a picture of an apple.

PB shakes his head. "Try again."

Two more times, and I still can't match the picture with the word. Strike three. I'm out. I chuck the card across the room and turn away.

PB unwraps something. I hear a candy wrapper crinkle.

"What do you get when you cross a snowman and a vampire?" PB asks.

"Huh?" I give him a strange look, so he holds up a piece of Laffy Taffy. He's reading one of the dumb jokes on the wrapper.

PB repeats the joke. "Give up?"

I shrug.

"Frostbite."

I don't get it, but PB's laughter makes my mouth twitch. He points at me. "Made you smile."

I stick out my tongue.

"You know, laughter brings you to a higher level of thinking." PB grins. "That's what your psychologist told me."

Great, now PB's gonna be my shrink, too.

"She told me about the secret weapons." He points a trigger finger at me. "I got another one for you."

I pop a Laffy Taffy in my mouth.

"Secret weapon #2." PB winks. "Laugh when you want to scream."

"Ha! Ha!" I say too loud for the library cubicle. Then I take the apple picture card and set it next to the word. I can't believe it. I'm actually right.

Jason
October 4

Today sucks. First I get a flat tire. Then I'm tardy. I fail a quiz in science, and PB grounds me.

I storm out of the apartment and grab my bike. I'm a block away when PB rides up on his bike and hands me a helmet. I spit on it and speed up.

"This is the perfect speed for BRAN," he calls out.

I curse and pedal like a madman. My tires whir with the speed.

I head north on Highway 10. PB's in my mirror with a sweet-looking Mustang behind him. I focus on pedaling uphill. A white Cadillac going grandma-speed is in the oncoming lane.

A semi comes over the hill, closing in behind the Cadillac. I watch everything like it's happening in slow motion. The semi driver blasts his horn, then swerves into my lane. Right into the path of the Mustang.

Brakes screech.

PB yells.

I hit the ditch without thinking. I bump down several feet before I fly off my seat. The semi doesn't stop. The Mustang driver screams cuss words out his window, while the grandma in the Cadillac drives on without a clue.

PB flies down after me on his bike. He jumps off and grabs me in a huge bear hug. Terror fills his eyes.

He doesn't let go of me. Not for a long time.

I stare at the packing disaster on my floor. Somehow Jason convinced my parents to let me camp with him and his dad over the weekend.

"When'd the tornado hit?" Mom stands in the doorway. Her McDonald's uniform smells like grease.

T-shirts are littered around me.

She pulls a cigarette from her pocket. "I'm going to bed."

I need help. At the hospital, everything was labeled with pictures or coordinated by color. The therapists gave my parents some ideas, but Mom's too busy, and Dad checked out once he lost his job.

Jason knocks on my door. "You ready?" He sees the mess. "What happened?"

I can't get the words out.

"Never mind." Jason shoves clothes in a bag. "The old man's waiting."

Enough said.

Jason heads for the door. "Let's go."

Maybe this isn't such a good idea. My family's messed up, but Jason's dad is psycho.

Jason
October 7

The old man is on beer #4 when Logan and me set up the tent. Empty cans fill the fire pit.

Logan stumbles with a tent pole, so I help him.

The old man sneers. "Brain trouble?"

I want to smack him.

Logan loses his balance. He falls onto the tent and rips the canvas.

"Stupid retard!" The old man explodes.

That's when I lose it. We fight like wild dogs. The old man yelling. Me swinging.

When Logan starts to shake, the old man gets this wild look and storms off to the truck. Logan looks awful. I grab our fishing poles, and we head to the lake. Hershey trots beside us.

"I'm stupid," Logan says.

"Like I'm Einstein." I try to make him laugh.

Logan trips over his words. "Brianna and Dylan have to leave."

"Leave?" Now I'm confused.

"They're moving in with my grandparents."

"Why?"

"Me."

I put two and two together. Less mouths to feed means more money for the bills. "How long?"

Logan shrugs.

Brianna and Dylan are annoying, but they're like family.

A tear leaks down Logan's face.

I don't know what to do, so I stick a worm under my nose like a long string of snot. Logan finally smiles.

It's late when we get back to camp. The old man's snoring, so me and Logan grab some chips. We sleep under the stars.

We leave when the old man wakes up. No apologies. Nothing. Just another ruined weekend.

Logan

"Hey, Logan." Jessie waves as she runs past the badminton nets. The girls are running the mile around the gym, and Jessie's in front of the pack.

"Heads up, retard." Austin swings, and the muscles in his arm ripple. The birdie hits me in the face.

I scowl. Just my rotten luck we'd get paired together.

"A picture would last longer." Austin smirks.

I want to smash my racket into his big mouth, but I can't even get the birdie over the net.

"Any day." Austin yawns.

I'm sick of his trash talk. I charge around the net, and Austin sticks out his foot. I fall on my butt—right in front of Jessie.

Austin howls.

Jessie stops. "You okay?"

"Yeah," I growl, and she takes off.

Austin slams a birdie over the net and scores just as Coach walks by us.

"Excellent," Coach says.

The little butt kisser grins.

I want to puke.

Jason

October 10

No school tomorrow. So me and PB take a late-night spin.

Maybe this biking thing isn't so bad. A crescent moon hangs in the black sky. I feel like I can touch the stars.

It's midnight when we get home, and we're starving.

"Wanna try my famous PB Special?"

Me and Laura beg for pizza when PB cooks, so I laugh.

A dozen eggs later, we eat omelets piled with jalapenos, onions, cheese and salsa. It's good, except for the gas. Poor Hershey.

Logan

The noise in the cafeteria hurts my head.

"Want to eat somewhere else?" Jason asks.

Before I can answer, Austin walks by and tips my tray.

Jason wails on Austin like he's a punching bag. He never used to stand up to Austin, but now he defends me.

"Fight!" someone screams, and a crowd grows. Catcalls fill the air.

"Break it up!" Two teachers run over and pull them apart. One gets a hook to the nose. Blood runs down his face.

They haul Jason and Austin to the principal's office.

Jason's the one who gets suspended.

Lunchroom justice sucks.

So much for a vacation.

Suspension isn't a party around PB.

Logan can't come over, and I'm grounded from everything with a cord or a battery. I have a mountain of homework.

Training for BRAN is my only escape from prison.

Yippee.

Logan

"Looks good," PB tells Jason at the library. He sketched four scenes from the story PB just read to me. Sometimes I forget how good an artist Jason is.

"Which scene comes first in the story?" PB asks me.

I look from one picture to the next. Three pigs and a wolf. PB said it was a fairy tale with a twist.

I point to the pig with the bricks. PB shakes his head. Jason nods his head to the left, trying to give me a clue.

"Without help." PB gives Jason a look. "Logan can do it."

"What?" Jason plays dumb.

"You're here to help." PB raises his eyebrows. "Not distract." He points to Jason's homework. "Get busy."

Jason starts to argue, but PB doesn't give him a chance.

"This bites," Jason groans.

I know exactly how he feels.

Jason
October 21

The weather guy on the radio this morning is a liar. "Slight" winds don't knock a guy down. I can hardly see because the headwind is so strong. Winter's gonna be a kick in the butt, and it's not even officially here. My socks are worthless, and I forgot gloves.

Good thing Laura's gone in the mornings because I run half-naked to the shower, stripping off layers in the hall—spandex, wind pants, two pairs of socks, a turtleneck and sweatshirt—but I beat PB. The loser has to make hot chocolate.

My skin is all red from the cold, so the hot water stings like a million needles until I get used to the temperature. I'm extra sore because PB's pushing me to build our speed.

"Get out!" PB bangs on the door. "You're gonna use all the hot water."

I ignore him until he flushes the toilet.

PB's dead meat.

Logan

Brianna hands me her favorite stuffed animal, Mr. Bear. A tear slides down her cheek.

"What's wrong?" I kneel beside her and lose my balance. I'm such a klutz.

I sit on the floor, and Brianna crawls into my lap. "Can Mr. Bear stay with you?"

"But he'll miss you." I give her a furry hug from her stuffed friend.

"Mr. Bear doesn't want to go."

Even I figure out she's not talking about the bear. She and my brother leave today. Their bags are all packed.

"Bye, Mr. Bear." Brianna kisses his ear and runs out of the room.

It's not fair. Brianna's only a little kid.

Why can't my parents send me away instead?

Jason

October 27

The old man's out drinking, so I decide to make an omelet. Biking makes me hungry all the time.

The door opens. I'm dead at 14. The kitchen's a disaster.

The old man grunts, so I slide over my omelet as a peace offering.

He takes a bar stool, then leaps off after one bite. "You trying to kill me?" Apparently I overdid the jalapenos.

I expect a blow, but the old man actually laughs.

We split the omelet, and he remembers a story from basic training.

"This kid in my platoon got sick eating an M.R.E. and spent the night in the crapper." He shakes his head. "Next day he was bragging about how much he pooed, so we pinned a blue ribbon to his bunk and nicknamed him Ribbon."

I laugh so hard the jalapenos burn my throat. He tells more stories—about castles he's visited and German volksmarches he's walked, things I've never heard before. It's after midnight when I finally head to my room.

"Biking's paying off," the old man calls out. "You're looking pretty buff."

I stop dead in my tracks. I'm speechless.

Logan

"You ready?" Jason's at my doorstep before the first trick-or-treaters arrive. He's dressed as the grim reaper.

I pull on a bloody mask. Halloween's our second favorite holiday—right after the Fourth of July.

My parents are too busy passing out candy to notice our backpacks. Good thing. Otherwise, they'd ask questions.

"You got past PB?" My words come out slow—like always, even after four months.

"Barely. The dude's hard to fool." Jason rubs his hands together. "So who's the first victim?"

I point across the street. The woman with the big nose is always ragging on me about skateboarding too close to her petunias. Jason tells me to hide while he sneaks up to the trailer. Three pumpkins sit on the front step. He grabs the biggest one and smashes it in the street.

"Hey!" Big Nose yells from the door, but we don't stick around. I used to outrun Jason. Not anymore.

We stop, and I'm breathing hard. Jason pulls a paper from his pocket.

"What's that?"

"Mr. Fenton's address." He's the teacher who threatened to make Jason repeat math last year.

We walk two blocks over, and Jason points to a house with shutters. We're in luck—no one's home.

"Too easy." Jason eggs a minivan.

I toss an egg and miss. Yolk drips on my shoe. I nail it the second try.

"Come on." Jason flashes an ornery smile. "Let's pay Austin a little visit."

The houses get bigger the closer we get. Jason stops in front

93

of a mansion and outlines the attack. I don't catch much.

Jason tosses me a can of shaving cream. "You gonna help?" I freeze. A BMW pulls into the driveway. The bass shakes the car.

We're dead.

Austin and Mike jump out of the back seat and tear after us.

"Run!" Jason yells, but I'm too slow.

Austin tackles me. My head smacks the ground.

I brace myself for a blow, but Jason leaps onto Austin and knocks him off me. The two roll on the grass, throwing punches.

A police car turns onto the street.

"Cops," Mike hisses.

Jason escapes Austin's grip. He grabs me, and we hightail it for the trees.

"Hey!" one of the cops yells, but we disappear among the shadows.

"You okay?" Jason asks when we finally stop. A streetlight shines on his face. It's puffy from the swelling, and he has a black eye.

My head hurts. "I can fight my own battles."

Jason shoots me a look. "And win?"

I want to punch my best friend in the face. And even I know that doesn't make sense.

Jason

October 31

PB almost splits a blood vessel when the cops knock on his door.

"What were you thinking?" He lays into me as soon as they leave. "First you go around acting like a little hoodlum, smashing pumpkins and egging cars. Then you get into a fight."

I start to argue, but PB doesn't give me a chance.

"You want to play baseball?" He gets in my face.

"Huh?"

"Suspension was strike one." PB scowls. "The police visit is strike two. You mess up again, and you're gone. You can live with your uncle in Tennessee."

Now I'm mad. I'm sick of adults running my life. "I don't need you, the old man, nobody." I slam my door.

The phone rings. A minute later, PB knocks on my door.

"Leave me alone."

PB cracks open the door. "Can we talk?" He sees my bag on the bed. "What're you doing?"

"Packing. I'm not waiting for strike three."

PB takes a seat on the edge of the bed, and I lean against the wall. "Logan's mom just called. Logan told her you took a beating for him."

I shrug. "So?" That's what friends are for.

"So, why didn't you tell me?" PB asks.

"When?" I shoot back. "You were ragging on me."

"I'm sorry." PB lets out a deep breath. "I've never raised a teenager."

The apology from an adult is a first for me.

"Remember what Doc said?" PB is serious. "Logan's brain injury increases the chance for more head trauma if he takes another hit to the head."

"So, I'm off the hook?"

"No." PB's answer is quick. "Vandalism is still wrong. You had no business being in Austin's neighborhood in the first place."

I frown. "It's a free country."

"With laws protecting people and their property." PB gives me a look that says don't push it.

"Fine." I shift my weight.

"Thanks for looking out for Logan." PB slugs my shoulder. "I'm proud of you."

I don't know what to say. I've never heard those words before.

Logan

Nothing gets easier.
I practice the same crap over.
And over.
And over.
Nothing changes.
Stupid me will never be normal.

Jason
November 7

I'm on probation. My record's not exactly clean, so I should be glad I wasn't sent to a group home. Lucky me—I got slapped with community service instead.

So now I really don't have a life—other than cross-training. We finally hit the gym when the first snow fell.

Logan's been in a funk since Halloween. Nothing cheers him up. Not even my dissecting story. This kid in my lab group pierced our pig's ear. It was a riot, but Logan didn't even smile.

Logan

My parents are fighting again.

"Why are you home?" Mom stomps into the living room. "You need a job."

Dad ignores her and turns up the volume on a PBS documentary.

Mom grabs the remote. "Stop wasting your time."

"Stop smoking!" Dad snaps.

"Get a job!"

"I'm trying. I was at the library all day filling out applications online."

"You better get a *real* job. Something with benefits."

They scream at each other until my mom slams the door. The silence that follows is just as bad.

I wish I could move with Dylan and Brianna.

Jason

November 28

Somehow PB persuaded the old man to let us join his family at the farm for Thanksgiving. I've never seen so much food in my life. Turkey, mashed potatoes, stuffing, homemade rolls, sweet potatoes, cranberries, green bean casserole, five kinds of pie, brownies, cookies and cinnamon rolls the size of plates.

People and animals are everywhere. Me and PB's cousins ride the ATVs, have a hay fight up in the barn loft, explore the creek bed and check out the horses. Even the old man's happy. He and PB's dad are swapping soldier stories.

"Having fun?" PB asks me when I load up on leftovers.

I shouldn't admit it, but I'm having a blast.

PB knocks my cap off. "I'm glad you're here."

"Thanks," I say and really mean it.

I used to watch *Brady Bunch* re-runs and wished my family got along. Stupid, I know. But PB's family's really like that. Nobody yells or gets wasted. They hang out and have fun. I never knew there were real families like that.

Logan

I'm craving brownies. Mom never makes them anymore because she's too tired.

I preheat the oven and try to figure out the steps on the back of the package. We're missing eggs, so I go next door. Our neighbor runs a daycare.

While I wait, a kid shoots me with a Nerf gun.

"Dare you to shoot me again."

The kid ducks under the table, and I wrestle him for his weapon. Three other rugrats descend on me. Nerf darts rain down on my head. Another kid tackles me from behind.

"Okay, warrior ninjas. Time for lunch," my neighbor calls out to the daycare kids.

"No," they call out in unison.

I join the protest. Our war's just getting started.

"Stay for lunch," they beg me.

When I finally make it home, the fire alarms are beeping like mad. Smoke fills the kitchen. I shut off the oven and fling open the doors and windows.

I can't stop shaking. What am I going to tell my parents? I almost burned down the trailer.

Jason
December 5

I'm home alone with the flu. PB and Laura left me some meds and chicken noodle soup, but I wish my mom was here. In first grade, I put spots all over my body just so I could stay home with her.

Mom figured out my plan when the marker got onto her hand, but she let me stay home, anyway. She wasn't up for waiting tables, so we both took a sick day. We slept in and watched movies all day. I never wanted to get better.

Logan

The trailer still reeks of smoke a day later. My parents nearly killed me for my arson stunt.

My head finally stopped throbbing from the scream fest.

Sometimes I wish I was back at the hospital.

Things didn't seem so complicated there.

Jason

December 11

The old man brought home a real Christmas tree—something we haven't had since Mom left.

I find an old box of ornaments. Most of my past is a mystery, so it's like opening a time capsule.

A tiny nutcracker reads "Made in Germany." I move its jaw and remember the outdoor Christmas markets Mom said she loved.

I lose track of time. The old man falls asleep on the couch while I look at each ornament—a pair of baby booties, a little semi-truck, a miniature chocolate lab, a small fishing pole, a tiny soldier. I wonder if Mom ever thinks about me at Christmas.

The light hits the last ornament—a small glass angel. A small heart is etched on the bottom with the name Alex in the middle. I sit back, confused. The old man snores from the couch. His name is Jeff. Not Alex. Maybe I read the cursive wrong. I look again. No mistake.

So who's Alex?

Logan

PB surprises me and Jason with early Christmas presents. He takes us out for pizza and gives us each a camelback water pouch and matching bike jerseys.

I try to sound thankful. But it's hard. Doesn't PB know I can't ride my bike anymore?

Riding again is insanity.

Jason

December 27

Logan's at his grandparents, and PB and Laura are in Colorado skiing with friends, so this vacation is gonna be l---o---n---g.

I wonder if anyone's ever died from boredom.

Logan

"He's not biking." Mom raises her voice.

"So what do we do?" Dad shoots back. "Put him in a bubble?" They think I'm asleep, but I hear every word.

"Logan can't get hurt again."

"So we don't let him live, either?"

Cigarette smoke creeps into my room. A sign Mom is trying to calm down. "What if he gets hurt, Dennis?"

"Logan needs this."

My parents are quiet, and I wonder if my mom has wrapped her arms around my dad—something she used to do all the time. It was annoying, but now I'd give anything to see a little public display of affection.

"I miss the tough kid who feared nothing." My dad is so quiet, I almost don't hear him.

A tear slides onto my pillow. The old Logan's gone. He wouldn't cry.

"Doc really said it was okay for him to bike?" Mom starts to cave.

"If he wears a helmet."

She sighs. "And Mr. Bertholf promised he won't push Logan too much?"

I roll over and stare at the ceiling. PB wants me to train for BRAN when the weather gets better. Not the miles he and Jason bike. But a quarter mile, a half mile, maybe a mile. PB thinks I can build up to it.

I'm not so sure, but I gotta try. Anything to bring back the old me.

Jason
January 15

I hate it when you have to waste a snow day on a weekend.

Since I'm stuck inside, I grab an old album and flip through pictures. My mom stares back at me, her green eyes full of mystery. One photo catches my eye. I'm sitting on a motorcycle. My legs don't even reach the foot pegs. A tall man with a beard stands beside me. I look closer, trying to place the guy, but I can't. Then I remember the Christmas ornament. Is this Alex?

I want to ask the old man, but guess what he's doing?

    a) doing laundry

    b) writing poetry

    c) drinking

Gee. I wonder.

PB says I'm moody, but I don't care. I'm a teenager. I'm not supposed to make sense. My past is this broken puzzle, and I'm missing half the pieces.

Logan

I can't concentrate on my math. I want to be outside in the snow. Not stuck in a library.

"Time for a study break?"

"Huh?" No lecture for daydreaming.

"I'm thinking snowball fight." PB smiles.

Jason looks up from PB's laptop. "Are you serious?"

"Like a heart attack."

We pile into PB's truck.

"Can we sled at Cottonmill Park?" Jason asks. "That killer hill is awesome."

PB raises his eyebrows. Killer hills don't mix with brain injuries.

Jason turns red. "Sorry," he mutters. "I forgot."

If only I could forget. Last year I was getting major air on my snowboard. Now I can't even sled down a hill.

At the park, Jason scoops up a handful of snow and pelts me with a snowball.

"Hey!" I yell. Jason throws two more before I pack my first snowball.

PB charges after Jason. "I got your back, Logan." They kick up snow like cars spinning cookies.

I concentrate on forming another snowball.

"Uggh!" Jason falls, and PB pins him to the ground.

"Quick, Logan!" PB yells. "Get him in the face."

I stand over Jason and enjoy my advantage.

"Truce!" Jason squirms, but PB holds him tight.

I plant a snowball in Jason's face.

"No fair," he sputters.

Me and PB just laugh. Revenge is sweet.

Jason turns on PB, and I join in. My eyes water from the wind. We're soaked when the battle finally ends. We head to PB's apartment for hot cocoa. I miss snowboarding. But at least I got out of tutoring. And for once—life felt almost normal again.

Jason

January 19

Our BRAN packets come in the mail today. PB wants to follow the Oregon Trail, but we're taking a different route—south to north in a kind of hook. The Udder Way tour. Get it? Cows. The Midwest.

"We should ride in honor of Logan," I suggest.

"That's a great idea." PB gets all excited. "Look. Brain and BRAN are only separated by one letter."

"BRAiN Ride," I say out loud. "I like it."

Here's the week:

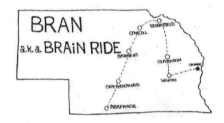

Day 1—Arapahoe to Gothenburg (54.3 miles)
Day 2—Gothenburg to Sargent (87.1 miles)
Day 3—Sargent to O'Neill (88.9 miles)
Day 4—O'Neill to Bloomfield (58.5 miles)
Day 5—Bloomfield to Clarkson (92.6 miles)
Day 6—Clarkson to Wahoo (65.2 miles)
Day 7—Wahoo to Omaha (35.5 miles)
Total—482.1 miles

The downside—we have a camper, but no driver. No driver means no Logan. Laura's gone to a music conference, so PB wants to ask the old man. That's crap. One good Thanksgiving doesn't erase the history. School programs, Boy Scouts, t-ball games—the old man never showed.

Why would he start being a father now?

Logan

I stare at my chicken scratch. A toddler could write better than me. I crumple the paper into a ball and miss the trashcan completely.

"Loser." Austin walks by and swipes it off the floor.

I try to grab it and miss.

"What's this?" He flattens the note and dangles it in front of my face. "A love letter?"

I lunge again and lose my balance. He laughs like a freakin' hyena.

"Jessie, Jessie, Jessie." Austin is so loud everyone can hear.

I curse.

"How sweet." He waves the paper in the air. "You scribbled her name all over your paper."

I want to deck him.

"Newsflash, moron." Austin tosses the paper in my face. "No one likes a retard."

He's right. Jessie deserves better.

I exhale. The old man's in front of the flat screen. He's on his first beer. It's now or never.

"You know how me and PB are biking across the state?"

He grunts.

"We're looking for a driver." I pause. "So Logan can come along."

The old man doesn't look up. "Can't."

I should leave, but I explode instead. "It doesn't take a detective to figure out why Mom left."

"You don't know anything, Sherlock."

Hershey whimpers in the corner. "She hated you. Just like I do."

"Then explain this—why was Mommy dearest out messing around while I was across the ocean serving our country?"

I want to put my hands over my ears and hum like a little kid. I can't hear you.

"She lost count of my beers when I returned, and I lost count of her boyfriends." The old man's breathing hard. "Her latest fling didn't like kids."

Alex? Her boyfriend?

"Guess what, Einstein?" the old man spits out. "Your mom chose him over me and *you*!"

I suck in air. If only the old man had decked me. It wouldn't hurt so bad.

"Leave me alone." I stomp off toward my locker.

Jason follows. "You failed a quiz. So what?"

It was basic addition. I don't want to talk. "Just leave."

"What if I don't?" Jason gets mad. "You gonna hit me?"

I beat the crap out of him last time we came to blows. But that was before.

"Go ahead." Jason doesn't back down. "We'll blame your brain injury and how you're so impulsive."

"Shut up," I growl. "You don't understand."

"No, you don't understand." Jason backs me into my locker. "You're not the only one with problems."

I curse.

"You're fine one minute and mean as snot the next. Try living with that."

I almost smack him. Instead, I duck under Jason's arm and storm off.

Secret weapon #3: Play hooky from the world for 20 minutes.

The resource class has a walk-in storage closet in back. Ms. J is helping a student when I come in, so I point to the back, and she nods.

I plop onto the beanbag Ms. J added for me. I got a killer headache.

"Hey, Logan." PB stares at me.

I blink. I must've fallen asleep.

"Ready to head to the library?"

I pick at a scab. "I failed the math quiz."

PB pats my shoulder. "It takes time to beat this thing."

Can I beat it? The question dies on my lips. I'm too afraid of the answer.

Jason
February 23

Mom's not coming back. Ever.

The thought surfaces as PB shakes me awake.

"Go away."

"You can't afford another tardy," PB warns me.

I roll over.

"I'm leaving in 15 minutes."

PB hasn't appreciated my attitude the last few weeks, so he made me double up on my community service. It stunk, but at least it's done. Now with spring around the corner, PB's itching to get back on the road.

I fall back asleep. So what if I miss school.

I don't even care.

Logan

I want to quit.
School, tutoring, life.
Everything.

Jason

March 6

Skipping school should've been strike three. It took a lot of begging, but PB finally agreed not to kick me out IF I signed a contract. Basically no more screw-ups.

The alarm rings too early. But getting up is part of our agreement.

Hershey puts his paws over his eyes when I turn on the light.

First day back on the bike since winter hit. I dress in layers, but it's not enough. The wind stings my eyes. Even the trains are cold—they screech every time they brake on the cold metal. I figure I might warm up if I put on speed. I pass PB, and the crazy dude is smiling.

Logan

PB won't let me or Jason quit. No matter how much we complain.

He helps me find an article in one of the library newspapers for my current event assignment in history. I'm too slow, so we take turns reading.

It's about biking. This ER doctor writes about the funeral of his son's best friend. The boy wasn't wearing a helmet when a car threw him backward into a steel manhole. He was dead at age 9. A shiver runs down my spine. Maybe I don't have it so bad after all.

"Hey, Logan."

Jessie's at the library. My throat goes dry.

"I'm here with my cousin," she says. "She has a research paper for high school."

I nod like a stupid bobble head doll.

"How about we take a break?" PB leaves, and I'm alone with Jessie.

The silence is awkward.

"So, you going to the dance?" she finally asks.

"I don't know." I almost choke on my spit.

Jessie frowns. I'm not so good at reading people anymore, but I think she's disappointed.

"Wanna go together?" I blurt out.

Jessie nods. Her face lights up, and I can't breathe. She's so beautiful.

She waves. "See ya later."

My heart hammers so hard, I can't even think. My brain is more mush than ever.

Jason

March 13

PB points out our first red-wing blackbird today.

"This isn't school, Professor PB." I give him a hard time. I'm more interested in the snow geese on the lake south of the overpass. Their white feathers remind me of whipped cream on hot chocolate. Warm thoughts.

I'm getting faster. PB tells me about these guys who raced across the country in seven days. Talk about a sore butt. He wants to enjoy BRAN—not make some record. The ride will be challenge enough. Fine with me as long as we're not last.

Logan

"This is stupid." I slump against the wall in PB's apartment. I used to bust a good move, but that was before.

PB turns up the music. "Would you rather have our dance lesson at the library?"

Jason laughs, so PB pulls him into the center of the living room. "Good. A volunteer."

It's my turn to howl with laughter. Jason flips me off.

PB struts around the room like he's on *Dancing with the Stars*.

Jason shakes his head. "You call that dancing?"

"Think you can do better?" PB challenges.

"Heck, yeah." Jason hooks up his iPod to the speaker. "If you change this lame music."

PB crosses his arms, and Jason breaks out with his best hip hop moves. The two go back and forth like fighters on a dance floor. I join them before I realize what I'm doing.

"Go, Logan. Go, Logan," Jason chants, and PB joins in.

I spin around, finding my rhythm. A smile creeps onto my lips. Now if only I can do the same around Jessie.

Jason

March 16

"We got up before sunrise to watch a bunch of birds?" My protests die when PB starts his truck. I lean back against the seat and close my eyes. The Sandhill Cranes come here every spring. Big deal.

Professor PB tosses me a migration map. I pretend to snore.

"Wake up." He punches me in the shoulder when we pull up at Ft. Kearny.

"People come from all over the world to see the cranes take off in the morning."

PB won't shut up, so I stare at his stupid map. Picture a huge hourglass with the neck going through Nebraska. The cranes winter in the south, then fly to a 50-mile stretch along the Platte River. They fatten up for a few weeks and fly north to breed—something they've done for centuries.

It's still dark when we park and head for the old railroad bridge. PB hands me his binoculars and points to a large flock roosting in the middle of the river. They like the sandbars because they see their predators better.

I don't tell PB, but I wish I had my sketchbook. At sunrise, thousands of cranes take off. Their cries echo through the air. Black silhouettes stand out against the pink and orange sky. I have to catch my breath. It's way cool. Right up there with the eagles at the canal.

Logan

Jason's the smart one. He's not going to the dance. I run my hand through my hair for the millionth time. At least it's finally growing back.

"Hey, Logan."

Too late to bail. Jessie meets me at the school. She's wearing a sleeveless dress.

"You look nice," I squeak like a rubber duck.

She smiles. "Ready to go in?"

We follow the music to the gym. I stuff my hands in my pockets. A fish out of water would look more natural.

"Want something to drink?" Jessie asks.

Anything to avoid dancing.

We're drinking punch when a slow song starts. Jessie looks at the dance floor, then me.

Even I figure out she wants to dance. Maybe I can bolt for the bathroom.

"I love this song." Jessie hums along.

"Uh, you want to dance?" I stutter like an idiot. I need my notes from PB and Jason.

Jessie nods, and we shuffle to the dance floor. I step on her foot, then knock her in the head. Not the smoothest start.

"Sorry," I mutter. My heart's beating like a conga drum on steroids.

The music changes to a line dance. Not good.

"Come on. It'll be fun."

Easy for her to say. I get confused making PB&J.

"I'll help you." Jessie grabs my hand.

My brain can't keep up. The group goes right; I go left. I bump into Jessie and set off human dominos.

My head's killing me. I run outside to escape.

"Logan?" Jessie calls out.

I can't hide, so I sit on the curb.

"Anyone sitting here?" She doesn't wait for me to answer.

A dog barks from someone's yard.

"I had fun tonight."

"You don't have to lie."

"I'm serious."

I chuck a pebble into the parking lot.

"Truth is, I admire you." Her voice is gentle.

I don't hide my surprise. "Why?"

Jessie's smile melts some of the hurt. "Because you didn't give up."

I don't know what to say.

That's when she kisses me on the cheek, and everything bad in my world suddenly seems right.

Jason

March 23

Grain elevators mess with my mind. I see one ahead and think we're close to town, but it's a mirage. You bike forever until you actually reach civilization.

Today PB convinced me to try a half century. Fifty miles is a lot of pedaling.

I want to capture everything on paper. An ostrich on an exotic animal farm, a great blue heron in an irrigation ditch and the wild Mustangs at the adoption center north of Elm Creek. Their eyes flicker with the same fierceness I see in Logan on the toughest days. The accident took a lot, but it didn't break his spirit.

Logan

PB takes me and Jason to a bicycle safety rodeo. A truck is loaded with free helmets, and shop guys inspect people's bikes.

One of my nurses is a volunteer. She remembers the day the ambulance brought me to the hospital. I get a big hug, and she asks if I want to be on TV. I can't believe it.

A small crowd circles around us. The reporter wants me to tell kids the importance of helmets.

Later when I watch myself on the screen, my words come out so slow. I'm even more of a retard than I thought. I hope someone watching won't make my mistake.

Jason

April 3

Rain trickles through the slats in my helmet. I forgot to stick my rain jacket inside my handlebar bag. A truck sprays us. It's hard enough on dry days when semi-trucks pass because the wind block creates a vacuum. Leaving it can knock you down. When it's wet and windy, the force is dangerous. My tires swerve. I almost wipe out.

Sometimes I think I'm as crazy as PB.

Logan

My bike leans against the wall in the shed where it's been since the accident. I take a deep breath and push it outside.

"You ready?" PB calls from the street. Jason races by and does a manual off the curb. Show-off.

PB pats the seat. "They say you never forget how to ride a bike."

I have my doubts. I grip the handlebars, and the frame wobbles underneath me.

PB steadies me. "Find your balance."

I don't know. Even if I can't remember the accident, I don't want a repeat of the last few months.

"I'll run alongside you," PB says.

Mom takes a drag from her cigarette and watches from the porch. She's not happy.

"You can do it." PB is way too enthusiastic.

Jason whizzes by. "Come on, Logan. Just try it."

I exhale and push off. The bike wobbles.

"Steady," PB calls out. I catch myself, but the next time, I'm not so lucky. I fall and scrape up my hands.

PB helps me to my feet. "You had it, Logan."

I wipe blood across my shirt and get back on the bike. Pedal. Steer. Watch the road.

PB and Jason jump up and down, cheering.

I scream into the wind rushing past my face. I'm doing it. I'm actually biking.

I'm a little winded after circling the block, but I can't quit grinning. I'm riding my bike!

Jason

April 13

You can hear frogs croaking in wetland ditches for miles on a bike. It's amazing in one spot, considering the fire there last fall.

"Nature's way of cleaning itself." Professor PB can't shut up. "Like life. We gotta go through hard stuff to make us stronger."

Maybe, but that doesn't make it easier.

We pass a farmhouse, and I see a yellow lab out front. Five little pups play beside her in the grass. On my 5th birthday, I woke up to a small tongue licking my face. Hershey was the last gift I got from my mom. Me and him haven't been separated since.

Logan

PB's insane—he's convinced I can bike around town.

"You can do it," he says, and Jason agrees.

I have to concentrate. Pedal. Steer. Watch the road. My muscles tense up every time a car passes.

"You okay?" PB asks.

I nod. Pedal. Steer. Watch the road. I'm so nervous.

The road has a slight incline, so I pedal harder. Sweat drips down my back. Jason beats me to the top. Before the accident, I would've smoked him.

"You're not in a race," PB tells me.

I grit my teeth. Then how come it feels like a competition?

I'm out of breath when I make it to the top.

"Way to go." PB slaps me on the back.

Jason frowns. "We haven't even gone half a mile."

PB shoots him a look, and Jason speeds off.

"Ignore him," PB tells me. "You did awesome."

My heart's still racing. "Can we rest?"

There's a park across the street. I feel like such a wuss.

PB leans his bike against a tree trunk and stretches his hamstrings. I lay down in the grass.

Pretty soon, PB's shaking me awake. "Your mom's gonna send out a search party. We both dozed off."

I pedal faster, but traffic is heavier. My brain's on overdrive.

Jason waits for me when I get home. "Where were you?"

"What do you care?"

"I was a jerk, okay. But you got me worried when you didn't come back."

"Okay, Mom," I tease back.

Jason raps my helmet, and I smack his shoulder. We've been through too much to call it quits.

Jason

April 22

Hills. Hills. Hills. The route to Ord is killing me. It's about 65 miles north, so Laura's going to bring the truck for the trip home. You can hear the *click, click, click* of our gears as we shift into low on the uphill and shift back again on the downhill. I yell at the top of my lungs and race PB to the bottom.

I'm gonna know every bird in the state by the end of our ride. Finches, killdeers, meadowlarks—Professor PB points out every kind. When we cross the Middle Loup River, two long-necked birds hang out on this log with their wings outspread.

"The anhinga are sunbathing," PB says. "Their feathers aren't water repellent."

We meet up for pizza with Laura. After about 10 trips through the buffet and a few stares, I crawl into the back seat of PB's truck. I'm asleep before he starts the engine.

Logan

"Can I have your attention?" PB's voice booms over the PA system at school.

Ms. J hushes our class.

"As you know, Logan Bailey was in a bike accident this past summer."

I freeze at the sound of my name. All eyes turn toward me.

"His best friend, Jason Johnson, and I have been training to bike across the state in a few weeks." PB says more, but I don't catch much until the end.

"Things have been tough for Logan's family. BRAN isn't really a charity ride, but we're accepting donations to help with Logan's medical bills."

Heat burns my cheeks. I don't know what to say.

Ms. J claps her hands. "Logan, that's wonderful."

I'm blown away. My dad says we don't need any handouts. But my family needs help. A lot.

Jason

May 8

Austin corners me in the hall after PB's announcement. "How's a loser and a retard gonna bike 500 miles?"

I want to spit in his face, but PB will kill me if I get in another fight. "Can you bike 50 miles?"

"Like it's harder than football or track." Austin and Mike laugh.

"How about a race then, Mr. Football?"

Austin's crowd grows quiet.

"Fifty miles. To Funk and back."

Austin sticks out his hand. "Saturday."

"Saturday." I tighten my grip. For once I'm not going to be the loser.

Logan

Jessie wants to go to the movies, so my mom drops us off at the theater. I order a popcorn combo with two drinks.

"That'll be $12.75," the guy behind the counter says.

I pull out my wallet and hope I get it right. PB's been working with me on counting money, but I still mess up.

A line grows behind me. I break into a sweat.

Jessie smiles, but I feel like a moron. I hand over two coins with the bills.

"I need three quarters."

I thrust out a handful of change, and the guy takes a quarter. If Jessie thinks I'm an idiot, she doesn't say anything. I'm relieved when I can finally hide in the dark theater.

Halfway through the movie, our fingers brush against each other. I reach out to hold Jessie's hand, and she smiles at me.

Life is good until I have to use the bathroom. Then I can't remember which theater I left. I panic. There are 13 theaters. I try the closest two. Both are wrong. The guy from the concessions walks by with a sweeper.

"Is everything okay?" he asks.

My face burns. "Uh, yeah." I hurry into another theater—also wrong. I slump against the wall. I'm such an idiot.

Jessie's voice reaches me. She's out in the hall, looking for me. The popcorn guy points to my door.

I can't hide anymore. I exit the wrong theater back into the hall.

"Logan!" Jessie exclaims. "Are you okay?"

The popcorn guy doesn't even pretend not to stare. His eyes bore into me.

"I don't feel so good," I mutter.

It's not a total lie. I'm sick of my brain injury.

Jason
May 12

It's raining on Saturday, so I dress in layers. I fix a couple eggs and fill two spare water bottles. Then I grab an apple, a banana, a few granola bars and some Fruit Roll-Ups for my handle bag. I strap on my camelback, pull on my helmet and bring an extra tube.

The old man is snoring on the couch when I leave. He'll be out till noon at least. There are six empty cans at his feet.

The rain turns to mist as I pedal toward the park. Austin is surrounded by his usual crowd. He's decked out in a new bike jersey and riding shorts.

I almost bolt until I see Logan. He sits alone on the curb with a homemade sign which reads "Go Jason!"

We knock fists. The sign would've taken him forever to write. "Thanks for coming."

Logan grins. "Beat Austin."

"Huge crowd, loser," Austin sneers.

I keep my mouth shut. Logan's worth all Austin's friends combined.

"Let's get this party started." Austin whoops, and his cheering section roars.

We line up and check both odometers to make sure they read zero. Somebody counts down, and we tear off. Austin's cheerleaders run alongside us.

My speed surprises Austin. As soon as his audience drops off, he gasps beside me. I smile. This is gonna be too fun. Austin has to work to keep up with me. I yawn, and he calls me every cuss word imaginable. We need a video camera. Then people can really see tough Mr. Football.

A cold crosswind hits us as we turn onto Highway 10. I'm

happy for my layers. I pull ahead, and Austin tries to draft off my tailwind.

It's real quiet, except for the sound of the wind. For once I actually miss the Professor's nature lessons.

The distance widens between us. Austin disappears from my mirror. If I could dance with my bike, I'd do the tango. Sweet victory music plays in my ear.

I turn onto Highway 6, nearing mile 15. I push 20 mph. I open my saddlebag and eat my apple as I pass through Axtell. Seven more miles to the halfway point.

Twenty minutes later, I turn at the park in Funk. The sun comes out, so I peel off my rain jacket. No sign of Austin. I wonder where I'll pass him. Two miles back, three miles, four? I can't wait to rub it in.

Back in Axtell, there's no sign of Austin. Something doesn't feel right. Did Austin bonk? PB's always ragging on me to drink lots of water and eat so my body won't run out of fuel to burn. He says bonking is worse than the flu. Even coasting downhill is a chore.

That's when it hits me. The cheating little rat turned back. He'd break his odometer and lie that he crashed.

Rage fuels my legs. I'm gonna kill Austin. This is my race. My win.

I'm breathing hard, cursing myself between every breath for being so stupid. Austin would cheat rather than lose. What was I thinking?

I bike like a madman. Ten miles. Five. Two.

Someone honks. PB and Logan pull up alongside me.

"This is between me and Austin," I yell. But PB's stubborn. He follows me into town.

I have to lose them. If I can beat PB to the park, I'll pound Austin before PB can jump out of the truck.

The hike-bike trail is ahead. Perfect. PB can't drive on the trail. I speed ahead, but PB figures out my plan. He's out of the cab the instant I hit the curb. *Pow!* The crazy fool dives into me.

I fly off my bike and roll with PB into the grass.

"Good thing you wore your helmet." The psycho smiles.

That makes me madder. I throw a punch, but PB blocks my fist. He tackles me again. I swing. He rolls. I swing. He ducks. I don't know how long we wrestle like that.

Finally I'm too tired to fight PB anymore. "Truce?"

PB sits on his knees. Grass sticks out of his hair. "I thought you'd never ask."

At school on Monday, I'm at my locker with Logan and Jessie when Austin strolls by. "Hey, losers."

"Oh, look." Jessie's lip curls. "It's the cheater."

Austin gets defensive. "My odometer broke."

"Whatever." She rolls her eyes.

Austin snorts, and his groupies laugh. "Once a loser, always a loser."

I give him the middle finger salute. Logan growls, ready to pounce.

Austin sneers, "Come on, retard. Let me have it."

I hold Logan back, wanting nothing more than to take Austin out. But PB would kill me.

"Only cowards can't admit they lost." Jessie cuts Austin down with her words. "Jason won the race."

The groupies suck in their breath.

"I didn't lose," Austin sputters. "I won."

Jessie links her arms between me and Logan, and we walk away, grinning.

"Anyone home?" I call through the screen door.

Someone groans.

"Jason?"

I take a step into the trailer, and fear freezes me to the spot. Jason's dad is curled on the floor in a t-shirt and boxers. He's covered in puke. A sickly yellow colors his face. I freak.

"Deep breath," I say out loud. I pace the floor, trying to think. I need to do something, but too much information runs through my brain.

Get help. The thought crashes through all the others. I start for the door when I see the phone.

Call 911. My hands shake as I punch in the numbers. Where is Jason?

"Hello. Are you there?" The dispatcher breaks through my fog.

My words come out jumbled, and I get all confused.

"Ambulance," I say over and over.

The dispatcher asks more questions, but I can't think. What if he dies? Jason will be all alone.

A siren screams outside. People bang on the door, then rush inside. Everything happens so quick. My head is spinning.

The ambulance leaves with Jason's dad.

I gotta find Jason.

Jason

May 21

I hate my old man, but I don't want him dead. I'm out cruising on my bike when Logan finds him collapsed on the floor. Talk about a loser son.

The hospital door opens, and a doctor looks out into the waiting room. Except for another couple, we're the only other people in the room. My knees get weak. Logan's mom squeezes my shoulder.

"Jason Johnson?" the doctor asks.

I can only nod.

"Your dad is lucky your friend found him." He smiles at Logan. "He has cirrhosis of the liver."

"Sir-what?"

"Cirrhosis. He's not getting rid of the poisons in his body."

My mind races as I try to make sense of the words.

"Your dad's spitting up blood, so I had to stick a tube down his nose. He also has ulcers."

I don't understand much, but I manage to ask one question. "Is he going to live?"

Doc nods. "The good news: Your dad doesn't need a transplant. The bad news: He could've been in a coma."

Logan's mom leans forward in her chair. "So what's next?"

"Mr. Johnson will be in the hospital for a few days," the doctor answers. "After that, he needs to quit drinking."

"Yeah, right," I can't help but snort. The old man would rather die.

Logan

Hospital waiting rooms are awful. People walk around like zombies. They wait and worry. And wait. And worry.

How did Jason hang out in my hospital room day after day when I got hurt?

I feel like I'm losing what's left of my mind.

Jason
May 25

I stare at the old man sleeping in his hospital bed. "I can't do BRAN. Not with him like this."

PB's quiet.

Check-in is next week. If I don't ride, I can't raise money for Logan. All our training's been a waste.

PB doesn't even react to my news. "I found us a driver."

"Who?" I ask, even though it doesn't matter. Not now.

"Logan's dad."

"Didn't he just get hired at the factory?"

"It starts in two weeks."

The old man stirs, and I take a step back.

"Talk to him, Jason," PB says. "He's your father."

I want to argue, but PB takes off, leaving me alone with the old man.

I stand there like an idiot. I'm screwed whatever I choose.

"Water." The old man nods toward his glass. He looks so helpless with that tube down his nose.

I put the glass near his lips so he can take a sip.

"You ready for the big bike ride?" he asks in a weak voice.

"I'm not going."

"What?" The bed creaks when the old man tries to sit up. "You quitting?"

"Quitting?" My temper flares. "I didn't train the past year to babysit a drunk."

His face hardens. "Get out. This drunk doesn't need your pity."

"Fine." I grit my teeth. "But tell me why first. Why'd she leave me?"

Hurt flickers across the old man's face.

My voice catches. "I'm her son." I break down. I can't help it.

The old man doesn't know what to do. I'm blubbering like a baby, and he's completely lost. Finally he sticks out his arms. I hesitate, but take a step forward. He grabs me in an awkward hug. I wouldn't be surprised if we set off a code blue.

When I pull away, the old man wipes a tear from his eye.

"Where is Mom?" Questions nag at me. "Does she ever want to see me? Who's Alex?"

The old man exhales. "Alex was her last boyfriend. The one she chose over us."

Us. I always blamed the old man, never seeing his pain.

"I'm sorry, son. She's never coming back."

The truth settles in my gut. It's hard to swallow, like puke that wants to come up.

It's quiet for several minutes. Then the old man takes his dog tags from around his neck and gives them to me. "For luck this week. I want you to ride."

I trace the raised letters with my finger. *Johnson, Jeff.* I try to thank him, but the words get stuck in my throat. I'm going on BRAN.

Logan

"That's our ride?" Me and Jason bust out laughing.

PB hops out of the camper his parents lent him. Circa 1970.

"Nice Hippie-mobile." Jason opens the door on the side, and we check out the interior. I didn't know brown, red and orange could be so ugly.

An hour later, we head down the highway. PB turns on the oldies station, and he and my dad start jamming to Bob Dylan and Paul McCartney. They sound ridiculous.

This trip could get interesting.

Jason

June 2

I expect all these biker types at registration—not a bunch of ordinary people from 25+ states. Ages range from 10 to 73. A lot of bikers have on bragging shirts—Cycle Oregon, Ride the Rockies, RAGBRAI in Iowa. Way cool.

Talk about tent city. Hundreds of tents cram the high school football field, including our blue and yellow one. Logan and his dad get the camper, but if it rains, that's where I'm headed.

Bikers double the population of Arapahoe in one afternoon.

People ride everything from recumbent bikes and tandems to mountain and road bikes. Me and Logan drool over half of them. Especially a neon green Y frame worth several grand.

There's all-you-can-eat spaghetti in the gym, then a meeting. Someone introduces the sag support team—Ranger, Cowboy and Buffalo Bill. They meet bikers every 10 to 15 miles with fruit and water. The nurse's advice makes everyone laugh: lots of Ibuprofen and ice, especially for sore butts.

Kenny—one of the bike shop guys—is the poster child for ADHD.

"Okay, BRANimals!" he yells. "Every morning, you need to do the ABC Quick Check. Air, brakes, crank arm, quick releases and a brief ride to check for problems. We want to avoid breakdowns."

Later, I can't sleep. The dog tags jingle around my neck, and I think of the old man in the hospital. I can't help but wonder. Would he be proud of me?

Logan

The smell of coffee wakes me up. "What time is it?" I stand at the camper door and rub my eyes. A figure takes shape in the dark.

"Five."

"In the morning?" I yawn.

My dad tosses me a chef hat he found when he got groceries last night. A matching hat sits on top of his head. "Pancakes sound good?"

It's too early, but my stomach answers, anyway.

My dad laughs—a sound I've missed. "You want to fry up the bacon?"

I want to sleep, but PB's taking down the tent. Jason comes out growling.

I grab the bacon and drop a strip into the pan. The sizzle makes me smile. I can do this.

My dad inhales. "Yum. Breakfast outdoors."

Jason stumbles to the table. His bed head makes me laugh. PB joins us, and the bacon and pancakes are gone in nothing flat.

Thirty minutes later, I'm in a sea of bikers ready for the mass start at sunrise. I can't do this.

PB reads my mind. "Remember, it's not a race."

Colors from different jerseys blur before my eyes. I'm trapped. Hemmed in by bikers.

"Logan?" PB's voice is distant.

My heart is a drum inside my chest. I flash back to the accident. I'm lying on the concrete. Still. Except for the blood, which seeps from the wound to my head. It's the first time I've remembered anything.

"Logan, Logan?" PB shakes my shoulder.

I stare into his face. My mouth is dry.

"You okay?"

"I can't do this."

"Look at me, Logan." PB gets in my face. "Secret weapon #4: Visualize your victory. You *can* do this."

Emotions twist in a knot inside me. Bikers shuffle into position around me.

"It's your choice." PB clips his foot into place. "You can pedal, or you can stay put."

My dad honks the Hippie-mobile and waves out the window. "See you in a mile."

I wipe my palms against my pants. Pedal or stay put.

One mile. Not much. Unless a bike accident changed your life. And you're sitting on a highway surrounded by bikers, wondering what in the world you're thinking. I must have a serious head injury.

Jason

Sunday, June 3—Day 1

Arapahoe to Gothenburg 54.3 miles

A shout. All 600 of us are off.

Adrenaline shoots through my legs. I adjust my gears and fall into a comfortable rhythm. Watch out, Lance Armstrong. Next stop: Tour de France.

Traffic is mainly farmers who come to check out the bikers. Soon a long line of bikes stretches out over several miles. Logan is so slow; I swear a hundred people pass us, shouting, "On your left!" as they leave us in the dust.

I mutter something, and PB shoots me a warning look. I pass the time by reading the dumb cow jokes and facts in my guidebook. It's in a plastic cover on the top of my handle bag.

The bad jokes:
1. What do they call a cow with no legs?
   Answer: ground beef
2. What do you call a heifer who wears a crown?
   Answer: a Dairy Queen
3. Did you hear about the bull that moved on?
   He pulled up stakes.
4. Show me cattle with a sense of humor, and I'll show you a laughing stock.

Equally bad cow facts:
1. There are about 350 squirts to a gallon of milk.
2. A 1,000-pound cow produces an average of 10 tons of manure a year. (Imagine being the scientist measuring that. Sick.)

I know I should be patient, but I'm thrilled to see the Hippie-mobile at the first mile mark to pick up Logan. Finally I can get some speed. Me and PB pick up the pace and even pass a few bikers. I surprise PB when I race up the huge hill going into Elwood. I refuse to walk one hill.

The first sag support wagon is up ahead, so we grab a banana and put on sunscreen. Then me and PB speed the next 11.1 miles to Eustis. I'm feeling better about things until Professor PB takes a detour through town for a German culture lesson. PB points out Wurst Haus and Der Deutsche Market to show me how pioneers from the old country set up towns like this. I don't care—I want to get back on the route. When I don't see any other bikers back on the highway, I curse. We're last.

Thirty minutes later, the sweeper van stops to check the route for stragglers.

Being last sucks. I want to throw my bike across Highway 23. I'm always last. Last at school. Last to be picked on any team.

I hate PB and Logan for making me last on BRAN, too.

"Maybe we should check on them." Dad looks at his watch again. We're waiting at the Pizza Hut in Gothenburg, and PB and Jason are really late.

My stomach grumbles something awful.

"What if something happened?"

I start to say something when the doorbell jingles.

"They're here." My dad waves to PB and Jason from our table. "Everything okay?"

Jason growls and disappears into the bathroom.

Dad and PB exchange a look. "He's mad because we're last."

I slink into my seat. It's all my fault.

PB reads my mind. "My detour put us at the end."

I grab my plate and head to the buffet. PB's just being nice. I'm too slow.

Jason comes up and takes the last two pieces of pepperoni pizza. He knows it's my favorite. Back at the booth, he's quiet.

"I'm sorry," I say, but Jason ignores me.

Maybe this biking thing isn't such a good idea for me.

Jason

Monday, June 4—Day 2

Gothenburg to Sargent 87.1 miles

I start the day with Ibuprofen. Today's route is one of the longest without many towns to break up the miles. After grabbing breakfast, me and PB leave at 6:15. Logan's meeting us later, so he and his dad are still snoring. I should dump ice on Logan. Being last got me a freezing cold shower last night.

The first 12 miles are great. The wind is from the south again. My fingers ache for my sketchbook every time I see an abandoned farmhouse or a horse standing on a ridge.

Some church ladies sell baked goods at our first sag stop. Heaven must be something like eating a still-warm cinnamon roll surrounded by hay bales in the country.

Road construction makes the next 10 miles bumpy. My knees are killing me by the time we turn onto a back road. Me and PB soar down hills, hooting and hollering. At the bottom of one hill, a creek twists behind an old farmhouse. Some kids playing outside wave to all the bikers.

Logan meets us two miles outside of Calloway. I'm hungry, so I'm not real patient with Logan's pokey pace. The homemade signs advertising food don't help. They're strung out over several feet. Moo-ve right along . . . for fresh fruit . . . ice-cold drinks . . . and udderly good food. PB has to stop for a picture of one group of signs. Need to potty? . . . We have johns . . . for udders . . . and no udders. Funny. Unless you're starving.

In Calloway, I gulp down lunch. I want to hit the road hard again, especially since Logan's back in the Hippie-mobile, but PB wants to help two girls who bike into town after us. Translation: We'll be last again.

At least the girls are cute, sophomores in high school. We

152

don't talk much till later. First is Suicide Pass—a 1.5-mile stretch with huge ditches on both sides. Then comes Democrat Hill. The guidebook says no one knows how the name came about, but I overhear a couple cracks about crooked politicians on both sides.

I switch into low gear and start the climb, while PB coaches the girls. I have to pedal hard if I'm not going to walk. So I push ahead. A crosswind hits me, and I grit my teeth. Sweat drips down my chest, and my leg muscles burn. My dog tags stick to my skin. I can do this.

When I finally make it to the sag stop at the top, I refill my water bottle and look out across Seven Valleys. Who said the plains were flat?

Fifteen minutes later PB and the girls reach the top. They down two fresh water bottles apiece. They wouldn't have made it without PB. It's worth coming in last again today.

The 21.2 miles into Broken Bow flies. It's fun to ride with someone new.

Jen and Natalie, a.k.a. Nat, are cousins. Their grandparents are following in a camper. We talk about music, movies, biking, you name it. Jen and me really hit it off.

Next is Sargent, 29.2 miles away. No wind, and it's hot, hot, hot. I take off my shirt and tuck it in my pants. With my shades on, the girls say I look like a California surfer. Jen nicknames me Dude. We get goofy and name other bikers.

There's Barbie and Kodak. She has bleached-blond hair, and he carries 60 pounds of camera stuff on his back. Her nickname slipped from my mouth when I ran into her at a sag stop, and the woman almost decked me. Long, red fingernails would've left a mark. Ouch.

Wild Man is Kenny—the crazy BRANimals bike shop worker. He whizzes by on a bike, then returns in the shop truck, giving everyone a thumbs up.

Sarge is our favorite sag stop driver who's always telling us war stories.

The funniest is Bones—a biker with a small science skeleton on the back of his bike. Every time he passes, the model looks like it waves a bony hand.

We get into Sargent about 4:30, and Jen and Nat find their grandparents. I hit the showers and actually get hot water. My body's so sore, I stay under the stream for a half hour.

When I get out, I call the old man.

After what seems like forever, I hear his voice. "I'm in a gown that doesn't cover my backside, and I can hardly pee without calling in the National Guard," he says. "Other than that, I'm fine."

I have to laugh. Humor's a good sign. The old man's full of questions about my trip. For the first time in my life, I actually miss the old guy.

Logan

I can't go faster. No matter how hard I try.

Maybe I'll leave my bike in the path of a semi-truck. Twisted metal would be hard to ride.

I want to quit so bad, it hurts. But then I see my dad smiling at me from the Hippie-mobile with his goofy grin, or PB telling me I can make it, and I can't quit.

I wish Jason understood.

Jason

Tuesday, June 5—Day 3

Sargent to O'Neill 88.9 miles

After breakfast in the high school bus barn, we hit the road. It's already hot, and it's only 6:30.

Logan has a rough start. He's in pain, and meds aren't any help. A baby could crawl faster. Watching the bike speedometer only makes the miles drag by slower. A half mile . . . three-quarters of a mile . . . one mile. The sun beats down hotter and hotter. Bikers pass in a steady stream.

I know PB wants Logan to be a part of the ride, but why'd we train so hard if I have to slow down so much for Logan? What's the big deal if I ride ahead?

When the Hippie-mobile finally pulls up, me and PB haul booty to Burwell. No sign of Jen and Nat. I could kill Logan—we're last. Again.

The wind picks up when we hit the rolling dunes of the Sandhills. Large cattle ranches stretch under an endless sky.

I take a leak in a ditch and get attacked by sand burs. I'm still peeling them off my jersey an hour later.

The afternoon drags on and on and on . . . with few towns and miles of barbed-wire fence that stretch forever.

Logan

Steam rises to my face from the beef stew. Everybody's so hungry, no one talks until Dad pulls out dessert.

"Is that peach cobbler?" PB gets excited.

Dad beams. "Made from a Dutch oven."

"And ice cream?" Jason actually smiles at me when I pull the carton from the cooler.

"We stopped at the store."

Dad dishes up the cobbler, and it's gone in minutes. My stomach feels like it could explode.

PB disappears and comes back with something behind his back.

"Ah-hem." He clears his throat. "I'd like to make a presentation."

For once, I'm not the only one who's confused.

"Logan and his dad deserve an award for all their support." PB pulls out a huge bra and hands it to my dad. "To the best sag support in all of BRAN."

Everyone howls as Dad straps on the double D and twirls around. Apparently PB found it at the lost and found.

After we clean up, Jason asks if we can go to the fair in town.

PB yawns. "Have fun. I'm beat."

I'm tired, too, but Jason pulls me along. When we meet up with Jen and Nat, I know why. Jason's in love.

Me and Nat have fun teasing the lovebirds until they ditch us. Then we head to the shooting gallery. Nat's aim is worse than mine.

We finish a round of bottle ring toss when Nat sees Jason and Jen. "Come on," she whispers. "Let's surprise them."

We sneak through the crowd like a couple of bad spies. They see us before we're even close.

"Anybody hungry?" Jen asks.

Nat's also clumsy. She spills her drink—which splatters all four of us, and her popcorn goes flying. Later, I find a kernel in my boxers. I smile. Nat's worse than me, and she doesn't even have a brain injury.

Jason

Wednesday, June 6—Day 4

O'Neill to Bloomfield 58.5 miles

Click, click, swish. UGGHHH!

Water sprinklers do not make a nice wake-up call, especially at 4:30 in the morning. I unzip my tent to get a face full of water. No wonder me and PB are the only two idiots camped in our spot at the high school.

We sleep a couple more hours, grab breakfast and hit the road. Twenty miles later we pass a fossil bed at Ashfall State Historic Park. Apparently some rhinos got killed when a volcano erupted. Weird. The only Midwest rhinos I know live at the zoo.

We meet the Hippie-mobile two miles outside of Creighton. I grab a Berry Pepper—frozen Dr Pepper and strawberry syrup—and speed off. Later we stop for watermelon at a farmhouse. Soon after, a crash test dummy on a bike welcomes us to Bloomfield.

Logan

My dad sticks his head out the Hippie-mobile. "Hey," he calls out. "Ride hard today, son."

Two bikers pass us, their gears whirring. Jason curses. Waiting on me kills him, so he speeds off.

My dad smiles. "I'm proud of you."

I'm speechless.

And it's not because of my brain injury.

Jason
Thursday, June 7—Day 5
Bloomfield to Clarkson 92.6 miles

Rain pelts my tent at midnight. I fumble with the zipper and run for the camper. Mud squeezes between my toes. I crawl into the small space above Logan's bed. I can't get comfortable and wake up with a sore neck.

It's still pouring in the morning. Everything is soaked. My shoes, my sleeping bag, my pillow, my duffel bag. Everything except a few clothes still wrapped in plastic.

I slip on my shoes, and water squishes from the soles. Biking in the rain sounds as exciting as taking a leak into the wind. And today's our longest day—almost a full century. Several bikers load their bikes onto car racks, so I decide to go back to sleep.

PB's in his raingear when I return from the bathroom. "Up for a little rain?"

I shake my head. "I'm sagging today." I disappear before he can say anything.

Logan's still snoring inside the camper. I climb into my bed and hear the dog tags clink together. I stare at the ceiling and curse. I want nothing more than to sleep, but I can't. I've come too far to quit. What would the old man think?

Fifteen minutes later, I turn my bike onto the highway and grumble at the rain. My conscience won't shut up. Not this close to the finish.

PB isn't surprised when I meet him near the Viking ship in Wausa. Instead he welcomes me back with a history lesson about the Swedes.

"Go kiss a Viking," I say.

He punches me in the shoulder. His look makes me glad I changed my mind.

Logan and his dad meet us at the fire hall for hot cocoa. I cinch up my rain hood, and we take off to Pierce. Twenty miles of steady rain. Fun.

As me and PB head south on Interstate 81, a ton of BRAN riders get flats. Wild Man Kenny is hopping. We escape, but Professor PB stops for a million pictures of wildflowers. He can't resist the way the rain drips off the petals. Prairie rose, coneflower, goldenrod—he recites their names like he's a freakin' poet.

The rain lets up, so Logan rides his bike the last mile before lunch in Norfolk. Then me and PB cruise onto Madison. Our last 25 miles take forever because of the hills. We top one hill, only to see another. Rain pours from the sky.

The sag wagon passes us twice, but PB waves the driver on. I count 15 bikers in the back of the truck. We've already biked 70 miles. What's 25 miles in the back of the sag wagon?

My legs burn, but PB won't listen. Instead Mr. Insanity starts to sing. "One, two, three more hills—come on bikers—aren't they thrills? Bran Flakes ain't no cereal—it's hill and hill and hill!"

When we finally roll into Clarkson, my bike odometer reads 96.5 miles. I peel off black socks (they were white) and discover prunes for feet. Under the shower, dirt runs off my arms and legs

163

in muddy streams. I dress in warm layers and dash to the Hippie-mobile.

PB shakes me two hours later. I'm starving. It's still raining, but the people in town rig a tractor taxi with a topper to take us downtown. I eat two T-bones and three baked potatoes.

Belly full, I head for the camper. It's too wet for tents. But the cramped camper is perfect. I sleep like a baby.

Logan

PB spreads the map across the table in the camper after breakfast. "You can do it." He traces his finger along the route from Dodge to Snyder.

I shake my head. "I don't know."

"Five miles," PB says. "The shortest distance between any two towns on the ride."

I haven't biked longer than two miles since my accident.

Five miles will be a stretch.

"Think about it." PB steps out of the camper to unlock his bike. "We have a few stops before Dodge."

"Mom's on the phone." Dad hands me the cell.

"Hey," I answer. "You headed to work?"

"I'm pulling a double shift." She gets excited. "That way I can watch you cross the finish line."

"Seriously?" I smile.

"I'm bringing a cowbell."

"Seriously?" I frown.

Mom laughs. "I'm kidding. But I'm going to be screaming."

My gaze falls on the map.

"Two more days," she says. "Can you believe it?"

I shake my head. Five miles. I'm a fool to even consider it.

Jason
Friday, June 8—Day 6
Clarkson to Wahoo 65.2 miles

Eat. That's what we do at every stop. This morning is watermelon in Howells, muffins in Dodge and brown bananas in Snyder. The organizers bought a truckload of bananas at the beginning of the trip, and they get mushier every day. I force myself to eat them because PB says I need the potassium for our ride. After BRAN—never again.

Logan's wiped out after he bikes from Dodge to Snyder. I don't even rag on him. His huge smile makes it worth slowing down.

A storm is coming, so me and PB fly the next 15 miles.

One mile from North Bend, dark clouds cover the sky. Lightning flashes, and the wind changes direction. My wheels spin without moving. Rain pelts my helmet. Me and PB have to slow down.

Main Street has two choices—the bar or the corner café—and it's hard to miss the Hippie-mobile. Logan waves us over to a table in the restaurant. It's total chaos. Wet bikers sit everywhere, two waitresses run all over and the cook is yelling.

Before I know it, PB's at the counter making hot cocoa and brewing coffee. Other bikers jump up to help, and applause breaks out. Two help with dishes, one busses tables and another takes orders. Bikers have invaded the place.

Two milkshakes, three hot cocoas, a stack of pancakes and two hours later, the storm stops, and I'm back on my bike again. The afternoon's a breeze, and we pull into Wahoo mid-afternoon.

I have my first accident, and I'm not even on a bike. Bikers get into the senior center free, so me and Logan meet the girls at the whirlpool. When Jen shows up in her bikini, I run smack into the wall and get a bloody nose. Logan can't quit laughing.

We walk downtown and see a bunch of bikers taking photos in front of a sign. I forgot Wahoo is the pretend home office of the *Late Show with David Letterman*. The four of us pose for a picture and catch the hayrack taxi back to the high school. We come up with our own Top Ten list for BRAN:

10. Don't keep wet shoes in your tent without a nose plug.
9. Garbage bags work better in the trash—not as raingear.
8. Don't become a waiter unless you actually get tips.
7. Helmet head is hopeless.
6. Eating 10 meals a day only works when you're biking.
5. Don't shout "on your left" back in civilization.
4. When you gotta go, avoid sand burs in the ditches.
3. Don't call other bikers by their nicknames.
2. Remember what bananas tasted like before BRAN.
1. Don't leave undergarments behind. They might become trophies for the sag support.

There's an awards ceremony in the gym when we get back. The funniest award goes to the road crew. Every morning they mark the route to warn of upcoming danger. Spray paint circles everything from potholes to road kill. One morning a string of small neon pink rings warned bikers of four dead crickets on the shoulder. Warning: Dead crickets up ahead.

The next thing I know, the announcer is telling Logan's story and calling him forward.

Logan

I don't realize the announcer is telling my story until he says my name. "Could Logan Bailey come forward?"

Hundreds of eyes turn toward me. Everyone's clapping. I don't know what to do.

"Logan, Logan, Logan." My name echoes through the room.

Jason nudges me. The chanting gets louder.

I feel my legs move to the front.

"As you know, BRAN gives away college scholarships to schools in the state, but we're not technically a charity ride."

I don't follow.

"We heard your story, Logan, and we've seen your courage. When BRAN riders found out your friends want to help with your medical bills, they took up a collection." He hands me a check.

The crowd erupts. "Speech, speech."

My muscles tense. I can't give a speech. I have a brain injury.

I stare at the faces looking at me. I spot Nat, and she grins. Secret weapon #2: Laugh when you want to scream.

"I trained a lot this year," I say real slow. "But not on a bike. I had to retrain my brain."

PB gives me a thumbs up from the front row.

"I wanted to quit. A lot."

Jason is smiling at me. I'm not the only one who's worked hard. Jason put in a lot of training days to bike in BRAN.

"I have a long road ahead." I look across the audience. "But a friend told me, 'You have to pedal, or you stay put.'"

The crowd stands and cheers. Nat's snort rises above the noise. I throw back my head and laugh till it hurts.

Jason
Saturday, June 9—Day 7
Wahoo to Omaha 35.5 miles

I follow PB onto the highway. It's our last morning, and I keep thinking about Jen at the street dance after the awards ceremony.

A horn blasts. I jump, swerving my wheels back onto the shoulder. The driver flips me off. I need to focus. On BRAN. Not on dancing with Jen. Or the way her lips touched mine. Focus, Jason. Focus.

"Glad you came?" PB breaks my daydream.

Somehow the flat tires, nasty weather and early mornings make today even sweeter. With the surprise check and our other donations, we raised more than $2,000.

I grin. "There are still 49 states left to bike."

"The boy is hooked." PB laughs.

Logan meets us for the last mile. We don't talk much. Even PB is quiet for once. We take the back roads into Omaha and turn at Chalco Hills Recreation Area. The smell of hot dogs makes my stomach grumble. Excitement creeps under my skin. I take the paved trail to the Visitor's Center and pedal hard. Logan's on my tail.

The three of us—me, PB and Logan—round the last corner. People sit on the grassy bank cheering the bikers as they cross the finish line. Without thinking, I search the crowd. My parents won't be here; the old man's in the hospital, and she's never coming back.

I look back at my best friend. His grin makes me smile. Logan got back on a bike again. It's nothing short of a miracle. And me—I biked 482 miles across the state. I can't believe it.

I'm almost at the finish line when I see him. The old man. I mean, my dad. He sits there in the grass beside Logan's parents and Dylan and Brianna and Jessie. He looks weak, but he smiles when he sees me.

I touch the dog tags, and he gives me a small salute.

The crowd is chanting Logan's name when I cross the finish line. I join in. My voice is the loudest.

About the Author

To spend more time with her best friend, Angela agreed to bike across Nebraska as long as she had a wider seat. Husband Will readily accepted, and they joined 598 other BRAN riders on an adventure chronicled in the fiction story *BRAiN RIDE*.

Character Logan had been hanging out in Angela's mind ever since a boy from the middle school where she taught crashed in a bike accident and suffered a traumatic brain injury. Early morning training for BRAN and long hours on a bike brought Logan's story to life.

When she is not riding or writing, Angela loves to travel, swim, read and spend time with her family. In the summer, she enjoys volunteering with Teen Reach Adventure Camp, a biblically-based camp for foster teens. In fact, a portion of *BRAiN RIDE* will help more teens attend camp.

If you enjoyed *BRAiN RIDE*, please stop by Amazon and write a review. Also look for Angela's other young adult titles due for release in 2013: *Late Summer Monarch* and *Tandem*. Find out more at www.angelawelchprusia.com .

About the Illustrator

Cyndi Mayer is a freelance artist and art teacher in Nebraska. Cyndi started Children's Art Studio in 1983 and has spent the last 30 years teaching children art. *BRAiN RIDE* is Cyndi's debut into book illustration.

Acknowledgments

Soli Deo Gloria. For God's glory alone.

A big shout out to my family:
Husband, Will—you've encouraged me from the beginning. Your undying support means everything.

Daughters, Meghan and Keely—you both warm my heart with your enthusiasm for my stories.

Stepson, Blake—do you remember making me smile after a big rejection at a writing conference?

Dad & Mom—thanks for believing in me.

Thank you to those who helped along the way:
Father Bob Rooney, who shared his experience with me after colliding with a garbage truck during a morning bike ride.

Christi Booher Galloway & her mother for their insights.

Author Kathy Mackel for her helpful suggestions.

Cheryl Popple & Lori Moore, resource teachers.

Carolyn Edwards, speech/language pathologist.

Nebraska Traumatic Brain Injury Advisory Council & the Brain Injury Association of Nebraska.

Ray & Sandy Weinburg, Jerry Baird & John Wupper, BRAN founders and visionaries.

Northwest Rotary Club & countless BRAN Volunteers.

Cyndi Mayer. Your "doodles" made the story come alive.

Daren & Nathan Lindley, Michelle Cuthrell, Melody Davis & the staff at Good Book Publishing. You're a dream team.

Kim Stokely, editor extraordinaire.

Crowdspring.com for your team of talented graphic artists, and Roy Migabon, the cover designer.